At

Peter's career in education saw him work at all levels from primary to teacher training. Head teacher at two primary schools in Devon, he later became head of a special school for children in local authority care. Before retiring, he taught mathematics at an academy in Somerset and now lives in Spain.

Dedication

To my lovely wife Alison, who remains as supportive and patient as ever while I'm writing and drawing. Also, grateful thanks to the wizards at Kindle Direct Publishing who helped sort out the complex formatting of the upload.

DREAMSPACE

written and illustrated by Peter Taylor

Table of Contents

Chapter 1 - Dreaming?

Without even kicking off his trainers, a tired and upset Marcus Flynn threw himself onto his bed, tucked his hands behind his head and shut his eyes tight against the day. Within moments, he was sinking into a troubled sleep, unwanted images creeping in from all directions. As he fought to banish them from his mind, he became increasingly aware of an unfamiliar presence. He didn't want to be bothered by it so he shifted his position to make it go away. But back it came, like some uninvited guest, penetrating with more and more certainty into his wandering semi-consciousness. Someone, or something, seemed to be watching and waiting. Whatever it was caught his attention, but he was tired and tried to pull himself away. Marcus turned over and drifted once more.

There it was again! He could just make out an image, too dark and faint to offer any detail. It was not frightening, as such a figure might have been in another dream. No, it did not seem to be a threat – more as though it was there for some definite purpose. He floated off again as his dreams continued, in which Marcus found himself looking around for another glimpse of the mysterious figure. His curiosity was satisfied, without warning, as the image appeared again, stronger and more substantial. Fully alert now, Marcus watched and waited, senses prickling and hardly daring to breathe. Whilst he did not feel exactly afraid, he knew he was trembling, perhaps in anticipation at whatever was about to happen. Slowly, the hooded figure conjured itself closer and raised its now partially visible face towards his. A cloaked arm reached up and pushed back its hood, to reveal a strong, kindly face.

Outwardly, Marcus hoped he appeared calm. But his palms were clammy and his heart began to hammer in his chest. Despite his efforts at self-control, he started violently when the figure spoke, even though it was barely more than an echoing whisper.

'Take my hand, Marcus. There is no need to be afraid.'

The stranger stood, waiting, right hand outstretched, palm upturned. Welcoming.

Swallowing his nerves, and with only the slightest hesitation, Marcus reached out and took the hand that was offered. At the precise moment of contact, a blinding flash exploded in his brain and he woke with a start, sitting bolt upright and trying to rub the light out of his eyes.

Already he was striving to recall his dream. Despite his breathlessness, he somehow knew that the sense of well-being he was now experiencing was everything to do with it. But try as he might, the substance of his dream was fading rapidly. As wakefulness began to clear his sleepy and tousled head, he became curious, if not slightly alarmed at the darkness which surrounded him. He wondered what time it was, and why he couldn't catch sight of the street lamps through the curtains. A power cut, maybe. He remembered the blinding flash. Involuntarily, he screwed up his knuckles deep into his eyes and peered at the blackness once more.

Slowly but surely, the alarm within him began to rise as his eyes finally began to penetrate those dark and sombre surroundings. He rubbed them again to be sure he was not mistaken. What his eyes now confirmed flipped his alarm directly to panic.

He was not in his room!

Heart pounding, Marcus shut his eyes and listened, hoping that his ears would contradict what he thought he had just seen. There was nothing in particular to hear, but the near silence was somehow different to the familiar quiet of his own room. A reassuring thought suddenly struck him. He almost laughed out loud with relief.

'Of course!' cried Marcus 'I'm still dreaming!'

But even as he spoke the words, Marcus, dreaming or not, realised he was not alone.

He sat still as he could, hardly daring to breathe. He became agitated and afraid once more, trying desperately to come up with a reasonable explanation for what seemed to be happening. This all felt far too real to support his recent dreaming theory. Almost too terrified to look, Marcus stared into the darkness and made out a dark figure standing across the room. It seemed unnaturally tall and lean, an impression perhaps exaggerated by the almost floor length cloak it was wearing. In a sudden flashback, he recalled the mysterious figure from earlier. One and the same, he decided. Just as in his dream, he was able to make out a face, strong and weather-beaten, which seemed to carry the cares of the world in its lines. The face turned more fully towards him, revealing a clean shaven, strong jaw. Above a large, almost smiling mouth rested a carefully clipped moustache which formed a perfect arch beneath a substantially hooked nose. Despite the fierce impression of these features, there was something calm and dignified about it – yet bearing traces of weariness, too. A pair of searching, though friendly, pale blue eyes were resting on him. At first, he wanted to look away or take refuge under the bedclothes. But those eyes were hypnotic and compelling. They held Marcus as if both lives depended upon it.

After what seemed like an eternity, during which Marcus felt he was undergoing very close scrutiny, the stranger spoke. It was the same, faintly echoing voice that he recalled in his dream, but now stronger, with more substance and clarity.

'Thank you for coming, Marcus. And welcome to Galidian.'

At the use of his name, Marcus stiffened. This had taken him completely by surprise, and the confusion he now felt must have been obvious to the stranger. Nevertheless, he stood quietly in front of Marcus, arms folded, waiting. Evidently, it was now Marcus' turn to say something.

'H-How did you know my name?' stammered the boy, uncertainly and, in any event, completely unable to think of anything else to say.

'There will be many questions my young friend,' came the gentle reply. 'But all that is needed for the moment is your trust. First, let me introduce myself. My name is Case.'

Marcus nodded not trusting himself to speak because of the dryness that had begun to clutch at his throat.

'If you will allow me, I shall try to explain what has happened to you, and why.'

Those pale eyes held Marcus, as if willing him to listen. By now, his earlier panic was beginning to subside, giving way to something closer

to curiosity. Comforted by the thought that all of this could simply be part of his dream, Marcus began to feel more at ease. He had nothing to lose – besides, he wanted to hear more from the stranger. Case, he reminded himself.'

'Of course,' he croaked, trying to clear his throat.

'I have asked you here, Marcus, because you possess something very precious. Something I know Galidian is going to need from you. Something I hope you will be able to give freely, when the time comes.'

'But I don't have anything precious . . .' Marcus protested. His voice trailed off as the stranger held up his hand. Once again, the eyes held him.

'May I sit down?'

Without waiting for an answer, Case turned to the wall in front of him and reached out to adjust the lamp. The dimness in the room gave way to a friendly yellowish glow which came from what appeared to be an old-fashioned lamp, bracketed to the wall. It hissed and popped merrily, apparently more cheerful on its new setting. Nodding his satisfaction too, a thoughtful looking Case moved to a corner of the room and picked up an ornately carved wooden chair. Although it looked heavy to Marcus, it was carried as if made of straw. The chair was set down beside the bed, and with a deft flick of his cloak, Case was seated. Once more, his drew Marcus' eyes into his own and began to speak, picking his words carefully.

'Your world is very different from ours. It is so different that I cannot even explain to you where it is, other than to say that it is not possible to travel to it in any way that would make sense to you.'

Marcus was listening with great attention and interest, head on one side. He wondered if he would remember any of this when he woke up.

'Very few people in your world even suspect that ours exists. There are also many here who have no idea about yours. And yet, here we are – you from your world and me from mine. That is plain to see.'

The speaker paused, searching Marcus' face hopefully, as if for signs of understanding.

'Despite the differences in our worlds, there are many similarities, too. For the ancient legends tell that long, long ago before even the dawning of our own history, we shared the same world – until the coming of Jorbeth. Some say that she came from the stars, others that she formed from the very substance of the very earth beneath our feet. But whatever, she did not like what she saw. There were those who were peaceful and caring, who asked nothing more from their existence than to be left alone to live it as they chose. There were others more aggressive and warlike, who preferred to take what they wanted by force. This led to quarrels and disputes, both within and between the many tribes that dwelt here. Jorbeth called the leaders of the tribes together, in the hope of establishing a lasting, harmonious peace for all to enjoy. But her efforts were in vain.'

Case paused, before continuing.

'From the very beginning, there were disagreements – over such things as territory, laws and leadership – until Jorbeth saw that there was but one solution. Summoning the tribal leaders once more, she described two worlds. The first, which she called Galidian, would be a place where people lived and worked in peace, sharing principles of equality and tolerance. The second, Earth, would be more suited to those who were more concerned with rank and title, and who preferred to establish themselves through the exercise of power. Each world would have drawbacks. Galidian, for example, would have to be shared with its original inhabitants - a varied mixture of creatures, possessing in some instances, abilities and characteristics beyond those of their human counterparts. It would not be a place for those who lacked courage and determination. Earth would also be a harsh place at times. For those who rose to a position of power and leadership, life would be pleasant enough, but very few would achieve this. For the majority, life would be hard, even though they could enjoy relative security under the protection of their leaders. The only real enemy would be their own kind.

Once again, Case hesitated, as if to make of sure Marcus' attention.

'Please go on!' he breathed, fascinated.

'Jorbeth sent the chieftains back to their tribes, telling them to explain to their people what she had told them, adding that each family must make their choice – Earth or Galidian. At the appointed hour, one world was emptied of its people, and two others began a new life. Your world, Marcus, and mine.'

'But Earth isn't at all like the way you describe it!' protested Marcus.

'No?' asked Case gently. 'Do you not have war, starvation, crime, injustice?'

Marcus thought for a moment. He remembered TV news pictures and a sponsored walk organised by the school for famine relief somewhere in Africa. All victims of a war-torn nation.

'Well, yes – I suppose so. Isn't it the same here?'

Case heard the question, but ignored it.

'Who is responsible for these terrible things?' he asked, instead.

Marcus thought again.

'I don't know. People, I suppose. Soldiers?' he replied.

Case smiled, but without humour.

'These are the casualties of war, certainly, each fighting for their cause.' he continued. 'But who controls these people, these soldiers?'

'Governments – I think,' he replied uncertainly.

'Do governments starve when there is famine, or fight in your wars?'

'I don't know,' answered Marcus. 'But they're on TV a lot, explaining things to people.'

'Yes,' murmured Case. 'Governments often have a lot of explaining to do.'

Marcus thought for a moment. He felt he was getting out of his depth and decided to put his earlier, unanswered question another way.

'Don't you have wars here?'

'No, Marcus. We have all kinds of hardships from time to time ranging from harsh weather to food shortages. But Galidian is a peaceful world and one we wish to preserve.'

'Mr Case, if I am in your world – Galidian – then how did I get here?'

Case threw back his head and laughed, revealing a set of even, white teeth as he did so.

'Just 'Case', Marcus, he said grinning broadly. 'And I will try to explain, but it's not going to be easy. Are you ready?'

Marcus nodded. He wanted to remember this in the morning!

'Things here in Galidian are not like they are on your Earth. For example, there is a small group of creatures here called the Brendel whose appearance is fierce and frightening, but who are in fact shy, gentle and friendly when you get to know them. They are forest creatures and were taught many generations ago that the power of the mind is far greater than any of us ever imagined. Indeed, it was through our contact with the

14

Brendel that some of us were able to search back inside ourselves to find memories from our distant ancestors and recall some of the things from our past that I have been telling you about. Things that had long been forgotten with the passing generations, from thousands of years ago. Since discovering these things from the Brendel, a few of us have learned to use our minds in other ways. This is, in fact, how I managed to find you, Marcus. My ability to 'see' into your world is very limited. It takes a great deal of concentration to find a way through all the interference created by the millions of other minds there, but yours shone out like a beacon. I have no idea why, but there it was! I discovered that, under the right conditions, I could enter your thoughts and even communicate with you. The next step was much more difficult. To actually bring you here, I had to find the right moment – when your mind was completely empty of all thought. Tell me, Marcus. Do you dream?'

'Yes' he replied. 'Often. But I don't always remember them.'

Case smiled.

'Just so. And there are those who say they do not dream at all, because they never have any recollection of having done so. But dream they do, despite their denials. Dreams are wonderful things, Marcus. Wonderful. Able to frighten, make us happy or sad. Just about any feeling you can imagine. They are also able to tell us things about ourselves, if only we could understand them. But sadly, the tangled language of dreams is known to only a few!'

Case looked serious once more, pausing before speaking again.

'My interest has been focused on the gaps between dreams. Dreamspaces, I call them. They are, in a way, endless – without time. These dreamspaces occur between one dream ending and the next beginning.

During them, the mind is completely at rest - inactive, so to speak. I used a dreamspace to bring you here.'

'But how?' asked Marcus.

'By waiting until your mind was empty of all other things. All I had to do was wait for your dreamspace and invite you across. The lack of activity in your brain allowed me to get through and place my mind alongside yours. You did the rest Marcus, by accepting my invitation. I could not have brought you here against your will.'

'So, you carried me here with your mind?' asked Marcus, incredulous.

'Sort of.'

'While I was in a dreamspace?'

'Yes.'

'So, this is all a dream!' Marcus felt disappointed, somehow.

Case waited for a moment before replying.

'Back on Earth, perhaps it is just a dream, Marcus. But not here. I am real. Galidian is real. And here, you are real too. You remember just now that I said dreamspaces were timeless. That is because everything that is happening to you now, and for however long you stay here, is happening in a single dreamspace. It might last just a few short moments, or . . .'

Case hesitated.

'Or last for ever. If and when the time comes for you to return to Earth, you will do so in the same dreamspace you left – and ready to begin your next dream. What I have no way of knowing is whether you will retain any memory of what has happened within it.'

Case relaxed in his chair, watching the boy closely. He seemed to understand that an important question was forming in his mind. Marcus was thinking. Case's words were nagging at him.

'It might last just a few short moments . . . or last forever. If and when the time comes for you to return . . .'

The words 'forever' and 'if' rang around his brain again and again, but their significance escaped him. Slowly, a doubt began to form in his mind. With a troubled look on his young face, Marcus finally spoke.

'Might I die here?' he asked.

Case closed his eyes for a few seconds. When he opened them, they were sharp and clear.

'Yes, Marcus. There is that possibility, for Galidian can be a dangerous place. I fear death here may well mean an end to your life in both worlds – though I cannot be certain.'

A long silence followed. It was Case who finally broke it.

'Marcus, I have to ask whether or not you are willing to help. If you do accept the challenge of what lies ahead, it will certainly be dangerous – but not impossible. If your answer is 'no' you will be returned, possibly none the wiser, to both your dreams and your world. It is your choice.'

Marcus looked at Case with a head still full of questions.

'May I ask what it is you think I can do – what it is you need from me? I – I can't even solve my own problems at home, let alone help with yours.'

Marcus was thinking of Prescott and Baines, a pair of nasty bullies from the new estate. Between them, they had made life more than miserable for Marcus and his friends.

Case's reply was quick and to the point.

'I don't know what threats or dangers lie before us, let alone how you can help. But I know it nevertheless – somehow. My senses cry out that something evil and foul is about to come among us. That is why I searched for you and brought you here. Other than that, I cannot explain. However, I am certain that you have something special – some talent or ability – and that it will be priceless to us.'

'But how do you know, Case? Has this kind of thing happened before?'

'Do you mean has anyone ever been brought from your world before? Or have we sensed danger at some other time?'

'Well, both,' replied Marcus.

Case paused, thoughtfully.

'As far as I'm aware you are the first – and perhaps the last – to enter this world from the outside. So, you see this is a new situation for us, too. We are not great explorers, content to stay within Galidian as we know it. Nevertheless, we are aware that new and strange lands lie beyond our own horizons, but apart from news from a few intrepid travellers – mostly sea traders – we know little of them. As for danger, I can only tell you that I have never sensed foreboding such as this before – nor been so absolutely certain in my life.'

It was Marcus' turn to be thoughtful.

'If I ask to go back, could you find someone else to help? Someone stronger and more capable than me?'

Case, once again, threw back his head and laughed. As his laughter subsided, he spoke with both sincerity and certainty.

'You are what we need at this time – of that I am sure. As for finding another to replace you . . . well, it's a possibility, but it could take much longer than I feel we have . . .'

Case waited.

18

Marcus turned things over. He felt very confused, understanding little or nothing of what was happening to him and having no idea what he might be getting into. Closing his eyes, he tried to think things through, but once more his thoughts were interrupted by the taunting, leering faces of Prescott and Baines. He drew a deep breath and let it out slowly. Something Mr Henderson, the teacher in charge of football at Parkford, had taught him to do to help clear his head after a knock. Something to do with oxygen, he remembered him saying. Without being aware of the exact moment it happened, Marcus found he had made up his mind. Opening his eyes, he looked up at Case. When he finally spoke, his voice was edged with determination.

'Well, if you think I can help, I'll stay.'

Case rose from his chair and offered his hand. There was both relief and gratitude written on his face.

'Thank you, Marcus! And once again, welcome to Galidian!'

Marcus took it, even though it completely swamped his own as it pumped up and down. The physical contact between them, the firm warm grip of Case's hand, caused Marcus for the first time to doubt that he was in a dream after all. And yet how *could* all this be real?

Releasing his hand, Case stood back. 'You must be tired. Sleep now, and we'll talk again in the morning. I am more than a little tired myself. Good-night!'

Case replaced the chair, slipped behind a curtain, opened and closed a door and was gone.

Marcus' brain was in utter turmoil. He began to wonder, if he went to sleep, whether all this would still be here in the morning. Secretly, he hoped it would be, but held out no real hope of the whole thing not being in

his imagination. For the first time, Marcus had an opportunity to look around him. His bed was large and the mattress rather on the lumpy side – but comfortable, nevertheless. The sheets were rougher than he was used to and the blankets woven from some sort of course wool. In the none too bright light from the lamp on the wall, he could not make out the colours, but they seemed to be mostly blues and greys and set in a pattern he could not recall seeing before.

Yawning, despite the excitement he felt inside, Marcus got out of bed and moved towards the lamp, intending to turn it down. Before reaching it, however, he caught sight of a curtain a little to the left of the lamp, somewhat smaller than the one he knew covered the door. He stood before it, hesitating for a moment. Slowly he stretched out his arm and pulled it to one side. It revealed, as he imagined it might, a window. He looked for a catch of some kind, but could see none. There was condensation on the small, oddly shaped panes. Putting himself between the curtain and the window to block out the light behind him, he wiped one of the panes. Cupping his hands around his face, he peered out. Although Marcus wiped the pane several more times, he could see nothing, except for a faint, flickering glow in what he supposed must be the sky. With a feeling of disappointment, he turned back into his room, adjusted the curtain and went over to the lamp. After examining it, he reached up on tip-toe and turned a knob. The flame dimmed behind its protective glass covering. Satisfied, Marcus looked back towards his bed to make sure that he could still see where it was. Yawning again, he climbed back in and buried himself in its warm depths. Despite the butterflies in his stomach and wondering what the morning would bring, he was soon fast asleep.

Chapter 2 - Awakening

Marcus stirred. Before he was properly awake, he found himself scratching at his arms and legs. He was itching like mad – all over! Dimly, he realised that he still had his clothes on. He was hot, too. As he slowly regained consciousness, events from last night's dream came back to him, one after the other. Marcus was puzzled, for he was never normally able to recall his dreams with such clarity and detail. He lay there for a while, eyes closed, still scratching and rubbing at the irritation affecting his skin. Finally, he opened his eyes, and slowly focused on the ceiling above him.

In an instant, he was wide awake, for the smooth, white expanse with its familiar cracks was not there. Instead, he was staring up at stones – *hundreds* of them! All neatly cemented together between long, sweeping curves, also made of stone. He remembered seeing something like it on a school trip to a castle somewhere in Wales. Then he remembered what his teacher had said about it.

'A vaulted ceiling!' a disbelieving Marcus whispered to himself.

He shut his eyes, tightly, before opening them again. The stones

were still there. He moved his eyes from side to side without moving his
head. He could see the tall back of the heavy wooden chair he recalled from

his dream, and the small curtain he knew covered a window. He had obviously not closed the curtain properly after he'd drawn it in order to see out, for rays of sunshine were slicing in through a crack. Millions of tiny dust particles rose, swirled and fell in a gentle, tumbling dance, seemingly trapped for all eternity in the brilliant shaft of light.

Gathering courage and crossing his fingers at the same time, he sat up, staring wide-eyed about him. To his left, he saw the large drape that he knew covered the door through which Case had left in the middle of the night. His eyes followed the wall from the curtained door to the window, past the chair, the faintly hissing lamp and on into the corner, where stood an unfamiliar looking piece of furniture. He supposed it to be a dressing table, for it had drawers and what appeared to be a thick, stone top. In the middle of this was a large bowl with a jug standing inside. Behind it, and fixed to the wall, was a mirror, but Marcus could see no clear reflection in it from where he lay. Now, he looked along the wall beyond the foot of his bed and spotted something he did not remember seeing the night before. A large wooden chest, bound with broad metal bands upon which he could make out some kind of engraved pattern or decoration. The chest was closed, fastened shut with a huge padlock, from which protruded a key. On the lid lay a pile of neatly folded clothes.

He could see nothing else in the room. Apart from the curtains across the door and window, and the lamp, there was nothing to break the monotony of the stone walls. Nevertheless, despite the lack of pictures and ornaments, Marcus felt just as warm, comfortable and safe as he always had at home. Pushing back the bedclothes, Marcus crawled out of their prickly warmth to the end of the bed. Looking down, he saw a rug, woven in similar blue and grey patterns to the ones on the blankets. He sat, edging his

24

feet lower until his toes touched down, much as if he were testing the water in a rock pool at the seaside. They liked what they felt, so Marcus firmly planted both feet. He stepped towards the chest to examine the clothes. There appeared to be an undergarment of some sort, a shirt, a pair of trousers and a cloak. Down by the side of the chest lay a pair of leather sandals. Everything appeared to be about his size! Resisting the temptation to try them on, Marcus moved into the corner to look more closely at the dressing table. It now appeared to be more of a place to wash, rather than to dress. In addition to the bowl and jug, which was almost full of water, there was a cake of something that felt and smelled like soap and a large, rough looking towel hanging on a hook to one side of the mirror. He tested the water by dipping in a finger. It was cold. Looking more closely at the mirror, it appeared to be made of a kind of shiny metal – he could not guess which – and although its surface was rippled, it reflected his face well enough. He decided there and then that the clothes and the washstand had been set out for him to use.

A quick glance around the room soon confirmed that there was no-one else about. He walked the few paces to the curtained window, stepping off the rug and on to the stone floor. It felt smooth, though not as cold as he had expected. All his attention was now on the sunlight streaming through the crack from the outside. Taking the lower edge of the curtain, he pulled it to one side, quite unprepared for the warm brilliance that now bathed him from head to foot. He blinked and shaded his eyes against the flood of light with an upraised arm. As his eyes adjusted, he could see that the panes of glass were dusty, except where he had rubbed them in his attempts to see out during the night. Moving closer, and peering with tightly screwed up eyes, he tried to look out – but it was hopeless, merely making his eyes stream in his attempts to penetrate the dazzle.

'Just my luck!' he spoke out loud. 'Last night not enough light, and now, too much!' His words echoed faintly in a way he had not noticed the night before, when talking to Case. He assumed it was caused by all the hard stone around him, whereas last night he had been on the bed, which probably helped to deaden the sounds of their voices.

Although the curtain was now open and admitting the brightness of day into the room, Marcus could see less than before. He knew he would have to wait a while until his eyes accustomed themselves before he would be able to see properly again. As his vision gradually returned to normal, he began the task of undressing, washing and trying on his new clothes.

First, he lifted the jug of water out of the bowl. It was heavier than it looked and Marcus had to use both hands. Carefully, and holding the handle with one hand while supporting the base with the other, he half-filled the bowl without spilling too much on the surface of the stand. The soap, whilst not resembling at all what he was used to, was perfectly effective and refreshing. Although quite unused to washing in cold water, he found it a surprisingly pleasant experience and found his skin tingling in a way it had never done before.

He turned his attention to the pile of clothes while he dried himself. Tossing the towel towards the bed, he picked up what appeared to be the undergarment and tried to figure out how to get into it. It was buttoned down the front and looked like a vest and a pair of pants joined together. He struggled into them, pulling and tugging here and there, until he seemed to be wearing it. When he tried to fasten it up, the buttons were on the inside! It proved to be just as difficult to get out of as it had been to get in. With a little perseverance, however, Marcus was soon satisfied that he was wearing

it properly and busied himself in doing it up.

'So far, so good!' he announced to the mirror.

He finished dressing without further difficulty, except for the cloak, which seemed to be the same inside as out. Laying it down, he fished around in his discarded jeans for the tortoiseshell comb he always carried in his back pocket. He gave his matted and untidy hair a quick run through with it, though another glance in the mirror told him that it hadn't made very much difference. He splashed some water on his hair and tried again.

'Better,' he smiled to himself in the mirror. The sight of his teeth reminded him that he should clean them, but in the absence of either toothbrush or paste, he decided it wouldn't hurt to give them a miss for once.

His clothes felt strange as he paced up and down the room, wondering what to do next. He eyed the key, still sticking out of the lock that secured the chest. He pulled his crumpled clothes off the lid, where he'd thrown them earlier, and heaped them on the bed. He took the padlock in his hand and turned it from side to side. It looked a lot like the one he had at home which he used, with a chain, to lock his bike up. But this was much bigger and much older. He stopped for a moment, realising that this was the first time since waking that he'd thought of home. There again, there'd been a lot of new things to take in, so he didn't feel too bad. He decided he'd better tidy up a bit, before anyone – if there was anyone – came in. Folding his clothes as neatly as he felt like bothering, he replaced them on the lid of the chest, just where he'd found the ones he was now wearing, and replaced the damp towel on its hook. Next, he turned his attention to straightening the bed. As he was smoothing and plumping pillows, his mind began to go over the strange conversation he'd had with Case during the night. Could all that *really* have happened? Could all of this still be a dream? It certainly doesn't feel like it, he told himself.

Marcus suddenly became aware that he needed to go the toilet. Very soon! He walked around the room, occasionally jumping up and down in an effort to make the urge go away. It did little to help, however, so he decided to look for somewhere to go. Another hopeful look around told him there was nowhere inside the room that would do. There was nothing for it – he would have to go out through the door he knew lay behind the large curtain.

He stood before it, trying to pluck up the courage to sweep it aside and go through, wondering what he might find on the other side. Uncertainly, he took hold of the curtain and slowly pulled it back. Marcus started back in fright, forgetting all about his biological needs for the moment. Staring back at him was a face, the like of which he had never seen before. It appeared to be half-human and half-beast and startling, to say the least, until he realised that it was a carving, set in one of the panels that made up the door. It appeared to be staring into the middle distance, not focusing on anything in specific. It bore the same expression he'd seen on the faces of the guards on duty outside Buckingham Palace – a sort of 'I've got much more important things to do than take any notice of you' look.

With difficulty, Marcus pulled his gaze away from the mask and looked more closely at the door itself. It was made of wood, panelled and covered with metal rivets. Fastening it to the doorframe to the left were three massive hinges, each stretching more than halfway across the door, between the panels. On the right was a large handle above a keyhole. There was no key. He bent down slightly in order to look through the small opening and was disappointed not to be able to see a thing. He decided that the key must be in the other side of the lock – the outside! Frowning, his attention returned to the carved face that still stared impassively past him. Its hair, forehead and eyes were, to all appearances, human, but from there down Marcus did not know what to compare it with. Its nose was broad and flat-topped, a bit like a lion's, and led to a mouth and jaw which could only belong to a strong, powerful animal. The word 'carnivore' sprang to mind. Somehow, Marcus knew that this could only be a depiction of something real, rather than just decoration for a door.

Nervously, and staying as far from the mask as he could, he gripped the handle and pushed it down. He was grateful that it made no sound as it moved. He pulled, gently at first and then with more force, but the door did not budge, even a fraction. He stepped back for a moment, assuming he was locked in, before realising that the door probably opened outwards because of the curtain. He tried again, this time pushing, and the heavy door swung easily and noiselessly open. Marcus held it, preventing it from opening too far, yet far enough for him to look out. It was a very curious pair of eyes that looked out, revealing to him a long stone corridor, dimly lit with a series of lamps much the same as the one in his room. Here and there, he could see doors. He wondered if one of them led to a toilet, his thoughts prompted by a reminder from lower down that he was still very much in need of one! There being nothing else in view, Marcus gave the door a shove and stepped out into the passageway.

As the door swung open, it crashed noisily against something on the other side. Next moment, a stool and whatever had been sitting on it went crashing to the hard stone floor. In the confusion that followed, a stumpy creature about the same size as Marcus and covered in long greyish hair, started upwards with a startled cry that sounded halfway between a yelp and a snarl. At the same time, it made a grab for its sword and a long, stout shaft with a wicked looking set of spikes on the end. Unfortunately for the clearly startled creature, its hasty efforts to right itself with speed and dignity were wasted, simply resulting in an untidy tangle of short limbs and long, unwieldy weapons.

The overall scene suddenly struck Marcus as funny, with his initial surprise giving way first to astonishment and then to giggles. The more he giggled, the more whatever it was strove to right itself – and the more it tried, the worse its efforts seemed to become. When its helmet became dislodged, adding its own spinning and bouncing antics to an already comical scene, Marcus became gripped with a series of uncontrollable fits of laughter. The unfortunate victim of circumstance, to the accompaniment

30

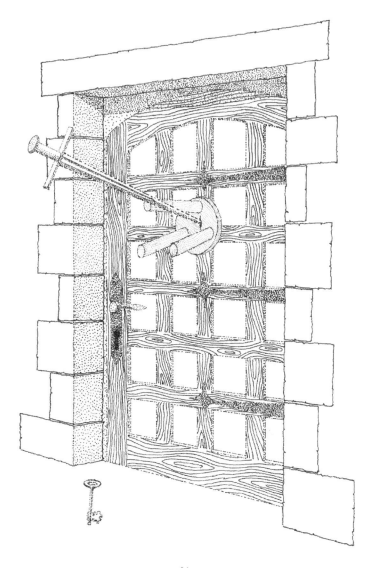

31

of some rather fierce sounding mutterings, finally managed to catch a hold of the offending helmet and return it to its proper place, albeit backwards. Its attempt to grab back the wayward spear, which had somehow worked itself between his legs and those of the stool, resulted in the creature heaving itself through a complete somersault, breaking the shaft clean in two and propelling the sword high in the air, neatly piercing the seat of the already airborne stool and embedding both into the door that had, just moments before, unwittingly caused all the commotion. The impetus of the sword's impact caused the massive door to close with a loud bang, as if turning its back on events in disapproval. Finally, even the key joined in the protest, as it fell, spinning and clattering, from its lock to the floor.

As the sword quivered mockingly in its new home, the only sounds to be heard were the heavy breathing and savage mutterings of one very cross creature, the fading clatter of the helmet which was making off down the passageway as if it had a life of its own and Marcus' valiant but useless efforts to contain his laughter. Finally, he managed to regain control and was now eyeing the fallen guard warily. Lost for anything else to say, he fell back on a polite greeting.

'Good morning!' he said, brightly.

'Luggerbugs!' spluttered the heap on the floor.

'I – I'm sorry if I startled you,' Marcus added, after an awkward pause.

'Startled me!' grunted the still seething sentinel. 'Yer near well scared me to death! What yer wanna go a-creepin' round like that fer, anyways?'

'I am very sorry – really,' Marcus added. 'I didn't know you were behind the door. And I didn't mean to laugh. I couldn't help it.'

Marcus could feel laughter bubbling up inside again, but fought it down, realising that another outburst would only serve to make matters worse than they already were.

'Here, let me help you up,' he offered, stepping forward with an outstretched hand.

The forlorn guard looked up, and, after a moment's hesitation, grabbed hold and heaved itself to its feet.

'Fanks,' it muttered, brushing itself down at the same time. It stared dumbly around at the mess. Probably wondering how being knocked off a stool could cause such chaos.

'All me own fault – shouldn've bin noddin' orf, like. I'll be right in it if Case finds out!'

The creature was now sporting a rather tender looking and visibly growing bruise on its forehead.

'Don't worry,' said Marcus, beginning to feel some sympathy. 'I shan't say anything.'

Eyeing the bruise, he added 'Can I fetch some cold water or something? That looks very painful!'

'No fanks,' it burbled. 'No sense, no feelin' – that's me!'

'Well, if you're sure – at least let me help clear up.'

The guard, for this was what Marcus now supposed him to be, looked at him fully for the first time and he saw gratitude in its eyes. Its face looked strangely familiar before he recognised it from the mask on the inside of his door. Mumbling his thanks again, the pair set about tidying up. It took a considerable effort from them both to prise the sword that had pinned the stool to the door. After the helmet had been retrieved and restored, somewhat painfully, to its rightful place, the only signs of a disturbance were the gash in the door, the torn seat of the stool and a broken spear.

Not a moment too soon, either! Hurrying footsteps were heard stamping up stairways at either end of the passage, getting louder and louder, until Case and an assortment of creatures similar in appearance to the unfortunate guard came into view. All of them were carrying drawn weapons.

Suspicious and alert, Case moved cautiously towards them, clearly expecting trouble of some kind. A moment later, having surveyed the scene, Case relaxed and put away his sword. His entourage followed suit. He moved closer to Marcus and put his hands on his shoulders.

'Thank the stars you are safe,' he breathed. 'When we heard sounds of battle, we came as quickly as we could.' He looked around again. 'Seems to have been a false alarm.'

Case turned to the guard.

'What was all the fuss, General?'

'Er, well, nuffin' ter speak of. Jus' an accident, like . . .'

Sniggering broke out behind Case.

'It was all my fault,' interrupted Marcus. 'I opened the door far too quickly and knocked him of his stool. It was an accident, just like he said.'

Fully satisfied that no harm had been done and at the same time interpreting in the damage, he addressed the sheepish looking General.

'We must take good care of this one, General. Great care, do you understand. He's very important to us, so mind you stay awake!'

There was more giggling from behind him.

'Yessah! O' course sah!' he replied, stiffening to attention.

'Well done, General,' he said, placing an encouraging hand on his shoulder. 'Perhaps you'll escort Marcus to my chambers when he's ready. We have much to do this fair morning.'

Case turned back to Marcus.

'General will see that you get some breakfast – we've all had ours. Then he'll bring you along to my quarters. There are some introductions to be made and many things to discuss. We'll see you later!'

Case turned, as did the others, to make their way back along the passage towards the stairways, not without a few curious backward glances towards Marcus.

When they were all out of sight, General spoke.

'Fanks again, young master. Fair saved me skin, yer did! I'm f'rever in yer debt. Anyfink I can do, jus' say – hear me – anyfink!'

'There is one thing – I really need to find a toilet. Is there . . .'

'Right this way, sah! I'll show yer mesself!'

Hurrying, he led Marcus along the passage and down the stairs.

Chapter 3 - Conference

On the way down to breakfast, Marcus ventured a question.

'So you're a general. That's very important isn't it?'

For a moment his guard looked puzzled, before breaking into a quivering gurgle that Marcus took to be laughter.

'I s'pose it is,' he replied, still chuckling. 'But it's jus' me name, like – General.'

I see. So I call you General, then?'

'S'right.'

This cleared up some of the confusion in Marcus' mind, for he had already seen that his guard was not really general material.

'Well, General, I'm glad you're looking after me,' he said, brightly.

'My pleasure!'

The pair made their way down a long, narrow spiral stairway that led eventually into a large, warm kitchen. A row of high windows along the far wall allowed angled rays of sunlight to penetrate the gloomier parts of the room. There were cupboards all around, some with their doors open, revealing unfamiliar fruits and vegetables, glass jars containing things that Marcus could not even begin to guess at and bags of varying shapes and sizes. A large iron stove stood against the end wall, pumping out heat. On it sat a variety of pots and pans, simmering and bubbling away to a tuneful rhythm all of their own. Above were more cupboards and to one side, a broad stone work surface laden with all manner of culinary items. This extended into the corner and back out along the window wall to a large sink full of steaming hot water. The draining board was piled high with pots, pans, crockery and cutlery. In the centre of the kitchen was a massive wooden table, clear except for two places laid at one end. Beneath the table were two neat lines of stools. The delicious smells wafting around reminded Marcus of how hungry he was.

'Late breakfasts, then, is it?'

The deep, though cultured voice, quite startled Marcus and seemed to come from the dark corner to the right of the sink. Blinking through the scattered light, he could make out very little. Something large and solid moved out of the corner, shuffling and scraping as it came towards them.

'Please be seated and I'll bring your plates,' it spoke.

It lumbered towards them through the slanting beams of sunlight, gradually revealing itself as it came – a large, cumbersome bulk supported by an enormous pair of clawed feet. Its short, fat legs were partially hidden by a rather stained and once white apron secured tightly around a bloated middle with a belt. Hanging limply by its sides were scaled arms ending in long, claw-fingered hands, one of which held a none too clean looking piece of cloth. As its head and shoulders emerged into the light, a puffy, overly large face with small, cat-like eyes was revealed. From somewhere in the middle of what Marcus imagined was its forehead grew a bulging, protuberant nose that hung right down over a gaping mouth. A mouth that was grinning from ear to floppy ear, exposing a row of stubby, uneven flat-topped teeth.

'Mornin' Grobwold!' greeted General, cheerily. 'What's we got t'day, then?' He sat at the table, rubbing his hands in anticipation, when he realised that Marcus had not moved.

'Sorry!' he exclaimed, rising. 'S'cuse me manners. Marcus, this is Grobwold. Grobwold – Marcus!' General sat down again, anxious to begin breakfast.

'P-pleased to meet you,' managed Marcus after a considerable effort. He had never seen anything quite so incredibly ugly and was fighting an instinct to turn and run from the nightmare that stood before him. It was only General's relaxed ease that stopped him from doing just that.

'Delighted!' boomed Grobwold, still grinning. 'Now sit down and make yourself comfortable. Be with you in a second or two!'

With that, Grobwold sidled over to the stove, swaying noticeably from side to side with each step. As it went, the creature revealed a broad, scaly back embellished with a row of spinal plates that gradually diminished in size until they were little more than bumps towards the end of its short, thick tail, the end of which just trailed on the floor. With some effort, it bent down, opened the oven door and produced two plates from its interior. A moment later, they were set down in front of Marcus and General.

'Good eating, my friends!' beamed Grobwold, standing back with another wipe of his hands on the grubby cloth.

'Ar good!' chirped General. 'Eggsies – me fav'rite!'

Eggs they were, with pink yolks and quite the biggest Marcus had

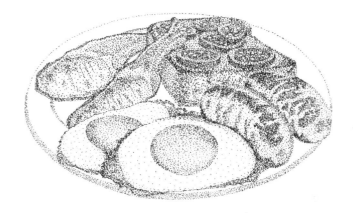

ever seen. Next to them were neatly arranged strips of crisp, lean bacon and a couple of plump sausages. The remaining space on the plate was occupied with a thick slice of buttered toast, topped with grilled tomatoes.

'Thank you – it looks delicious!' Marcus managed a shy smile up at Grobwold.

His initial fright had subsided considerably with the appearance of breakfast. He picked up the knife and two-pronged fork that lay to one side of his plate and tucked in hungrily. General had already started. In truth, he was almost finished, making loud slurping and chomping noises as he shovelled a continuous stream of food into his mouth at a quite unbelievable rate. The sight and sound of general's demolition of breakfast would have been enough to put most people off their food for life, but Marcus was so hungry and engrossed in his own plateful that he barely noticed. With a loud belch and a wipe of his jaw with the back of his hand, General sat back eyeing Marcus' plate.

'Want that there sossige?' he asked, leaning forward hopefully.

39

'Um – shlub – rurla,' garbled Marcus, his mouth too full to allow anything intelligible to come out.

Taking this to mean 'No, thank you very much, I don't think I can quite manage it,' the sausage was deftly stabbed and down General's throat in a single movement. A few moments later and ably assisted by General's insatiable appetite, Marcus' plate was empty too. Next time they ate together, Marcus decided, he would sit a little further away.

Grobwold returned to the table, carrying a plate of toast, a jar of bright red jam and two mugs of hot, sweet milk. Marcus managed one piece of toast while General cleaned up the rest. He enjoyed the milk so much that he kept his hands around his mug until it was all gone. General looked disappointed.

'Best cook in Galidian, ain't yer Grobwold!' General called over his shoulder.

'There's no more, so you can cut out the flattery,' replied Grobwold testily, coming across from the sink. 'And how was *your* breakfast, Marcus? What little you could manage to keep 'dustbin' there away from, that is!' He shot a reproving glance at General as he spoke.

'It was delicious, thank you,' replied Marcus. 'And I've had more than enough, really!'

'Are you sure? I could find you a couple of biscuits, if you like.'

Marcus shook his head with a smile, but General was alert in an instant.

'Cor! Bikkies!' Yummy-yummy-yummy! I love 'em!' he enthused.

'Not you, bog guts! You've packed away enough breakfast for three already,' retorted Grobwold. 'Anyone would think you hadn't eaten for a week!'

'I 'aven't' grumbled General.

'Oh yes! And what about the 'snack' you had before you went on duty last night? Best part of two loaves of bread, that was!'

Realising he wasn't going to get anything more to eat, General stood up from the table.

'No sense in 'angin about 'ere, then!' he pouted. 'Come on, Marcus. We'd best get over ter see Case.'

'Thanks again, Grobwold!' called Marcus, rising to follow General.

'A real pleasure,' he smiled. 'See you at lunch!'

With General still grumbling about being hungry, Marcus tried to make conversation as they strode along.

'Nice, isn't he?'

'Who?'

'Grobwold.'

'E's alright – fer a Wampy.'

'What's a Wampy?' asked Marcus, having to hurry to keep up.

'Short fer Wampurian. E's one,' he replied, with a backward gesture of his head. 'An' bossy wiv it!'

Marcus had decided to try another subject when General stopped abruptly outside a pair of imposing wooden doors. He rapped loudly and, without waiting, pushed one open. He beckoned Marcus through. Stepping over the threshold he saw Case, with others, standing around a huge table in the centre of a large hall. It was spread with maps, papers and all manner of things. At the interruption, Case looked up and started to cross the floor, smiling as he did so.

'Good morning again, Marcus! I trust you cnjoycd breakfast?'

'Very much, thank you.'

Just beside him, General let out a scowl.

'And how did you sleep last night?'

'Very well. And you?' Marcus replied.

'I didn't. There will be plenty of time for sleep later, but for now, there are more important matters to deal with. That is why the Albard are here and why General was posted outside your room last night. But more of that later – first, come and meet my friends, the Albard!'

Placing an arm across Marcus' shoulder, Case guided him towards the table. There were several creatures like General waiting there, all with eyes turned on him. The colour of their body hair varied considerably, from greyish white, through various shades of reddish and yellowish browns to black. Some had mixtures of two or more colours. They also varied considerably in stature. It was towards one of the taller ones that Case guided him now, an imposing figure with almost black hair and thick, strong looking limbs.

'Marcus, this is Trench, Chieftain of the Albard.'

'Welcome ter Galidian!' drawled Trench, looking him up and down with folded arms. 'Case tells us yer 'ere to 'elp.' He turned his gaze back to Case, as if wondering what possible use this stripling of a boy could be.

Marcus suddenly felt awkward and unable to answer the greeting. Case spoke for him.

'All in good time, my friend. All in good time.'

He walked Marcus slowly around the table, introducing him to the rest of the Albard, one by one. 'This is Richmane . . . Welgar . . . Hodun . . . Teshtal . . . Emdren . . . and Udiger. And General, well – you've already bumped into him!'

Marcus smiled at General, who, although embarrassed at Case's

42

little dig, joined in the good-natured laughter that followed. He smiled back at Marcus, winking as he did so, as if the pair of them shared a secret. At least, his earlier sour temper had gone, and Marcus was pleased about that.

Case became serious as he spoke again.

'The Albard arrived late last night after travelling almost non-stop from their homeland on the fringes of the Southern Wastes. It is a difficult and dangerous journey and they have done well to get here in just six days!'

Case waited, tight-lipped, before continuing.

'They bring disturbing news of strange activities high up in the mountains behind them, the same mountains that have always been a natural barrier between ourselves and the rest of Galidian. We call the region on the other side of the mountains The Shadowlands. Here, let me show you.'

Case turned to the table and slid a large piece of curling parchment from under a pile of other papers. He spread it carefully, smoothed its edges and weighted them down with a curious selection of mottled stones that he picked from a wooden bowl close at hand. A closer inspection of the stones would have revealed to Marcus that each bore a deeply grooved pattern, but he was much too interested in the map that now lay before him to notice. He loved maps, and this was unlike any other he had seen. It showed a landmass, delicately coloured in hues of greens, browns and mauves. Its coastline was dotted with islands, whilst the interior was finely detailed in different coloured inks showing rivers, forests, deserts, marshes and mountains. There were names written everywhere, some in a large decorative script and others in small, neat lettering. Here and there were tiny drawings of ships, towns, villages and bizarre looking creatures. His eager eyes picked out one drawing near the middle of the map, showing a single Albard.

Case interrupted his gazing.

'This is Galidian,' he began, indicating the whole map with a circular movement of his hand. 'We know the shape of the coastline because of the work of the map makers put aboard the sea-faring ships that leave Eastport from time to time. You can see how our land is divided by the mountains I mentioned earlier. We call them the Curtains.' His finger traced a large, 'S' shape from top to bottom of the map.

'At both northern and southern ends lie vast marshes. We know them to be dangerous places and keep well clear. These mountains effectively cut our world in two. On this side, Galidian as we know it. On the other side – The Shadowlands. Its coastline is well protected all the way around by mountains, swamps or dense, impenetrable forest. That is why we know nothing of its interior.'

'Where are we?' asked Marcus.

'Just here,' indicated Case, placing a finger near the top right-hand corner of the map. 'Stonefort.'

Marcus had to stretch on tiptoe and lean forward in order to get close enough to see where Case was pointing. To the side of his fingernail was another of the small drawings, this one showing a turreted, castle-like building with the single word 'Stonefort' inscribed beneath it.

'Is this a town?' asked Marcus, pointing to a collection of houses drawn closely huddled together on a short stretch of river between two lakes. He had difficulty making out the name.

'Yes! That's Middlemere. But come with me – it's about time you saw something of Galidian for yourself!'

Case turned away from the table and made for an arched doorway

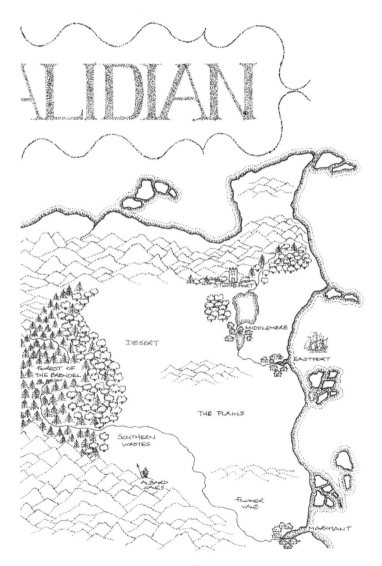

set in the wall opposite to the one through which Marcus had entered. Beckoning, Case opened the door and disappeared up a broad stairway. As Marcus reached the bottom of the steps, light from above washed down on him as Case flung open another door. He stood, framed in the upper doorway, outlined against a bright blue sky. He half turned, calling as he did so.

'Come and see, Marcus!'

As he reached the top of the steps, Marcus saw a wide, spacious terrace spread before him. Around its outer edge was a protective stone balustrade and beyond, an unbroken expanse of sky. He stepped forward, eyes narrowed against the light, until he could place both hands on the smooth, sun-warmed barrier.

'Galidian!' announced Case, with an outward sweep of his arm.

The panorama that met Marcus' astonished gaze was truly stunning. The balcony on which he was standing was set, at a dizzying height, into an enormous cliff. Virtually the whole horizon was spiked with monumental, snow-capped mountains, so distant as to be almost without substance, like some gigantic, unfinished mural. Their massive, transparent flanks gave way to a series of hill ranges, silhouetted against one another and deepening in hues of greys, purples and greens as they rolled ever closer. Huge plains swept down from the hills, both forested and barren, until they drifted into a colourful patchwork of fields interlaced with rivers and streams. Below him lay a vast lake, its surface so still that it perfectly reflected the pure blue of the sky, and clear enough to see through to its bed, at least around its shallow fringes, until the water became too deep to penetrate. A large river emerging from the forest joined forces with another before flowing into the lake from the west and out on the opposite side. On the banks of the river, before it wound and tumbled its way into a smaller and more distant lake, lay a town.

Marcus looked up at Case.

'Middlemere!' he nodded. 'And if you follow the river, you will eventually reach Eastport and the ocean.'

Marcus strained his eyes in the direction Case indicated, but could see nothing, save for meadowlands spreading towards the horizon obscured by the haze generated by the warmth of the sun.

'It's beautiful!' breathed Marcus, eyes bright and excited.

'And worth protecting, don't you agree?'

A shadow had fallen across Case's face once more. He sagged forward, looking suddenly exhausted. The whites of his knuckles stood out as he gripped the balcony wall, revealing the tension he felt throughout his body. Without warning, Case spun around.

'I have something else to show you, Marcus. Come!'

This was not an invitation – more of a directive. Marcus allowed himself one last look at the magnificent view before following Case back across the terrace, down the steps and into the room below. By the time he got there, Case was already holding something in his hands. It was a neatly stitched leather pouch. From it, he withdrew a smooth, black object that glinted dully in his hands.

'The Albard brought this with them last night. Have you any idea what it is?' Case set it down on the table, next to the map, as he spoke.

It was a perfectly formed sphere and seemed somehow to both absorb and reflect light, being smooth but not at all shiny. Marcus had a feeling that he had seen something like it before, but could not think where or when. He shook his head as he answered the question.

47

'I'm not sure – I don't think so.'

Case looked hard at him, before continuing.

'One night, half a moon or so back, the Albard saw strange flashes high in the mountains. Ordinarily, they would have put them down to a storm, but there were no clouds to be seen. It was a perfectly clear night. Next morning, they sent a party to investigate. When the expedition failed to return, they sent another, led by Trench here. What they found was both terrible and unaccountable.'

'The group had been set upon by some unknown assailant and slaughtered without mercy, their bodies ripped apart and charred almost beyond recognition. The ground all around them was blackened, showing that great heat had been used. It appeared as if they had been caught unawares as they camped for the night, for their bedrolls and personal belongings were scattered around the site. As the rescue team began the grim task of burying the bodies of their friends, they found this.'

Case paused, nodding towards the dully glinting sphere on the table.

'They concluded that it had either been put there or accidentally dropped by whoever, or whatever, was responsible for the slaughter.'

Marcus thought for a moment.

'Couldn't the Albard have found it on their way up the mountain?' he asked. There was a buzz of conversation around the table.

Finally, it was Trench who spoke, this time with a note of respect in his voice, rather than the half-mocking tone he had used earlier.

"Could be right, young 'un,' he acknowledged. 'We found it hidden under a rock, near one of the bodies.' Trench shook his head with the recollection. 'A terrible business,' he muttered.

'I reckon 'e's proberly right too. Makes sense!' added Hodum, who

48

had also been part of the rescue team.

'What makes you think that?' asked Case.

'Well, it stands ter reason,' he continued. 'Them remains 'ad been burned alive *before* being ripped open – otherwise their wounds would've been scorched too. But they weren't, see – all fresh an' . . .'

Hodum stopped there, obviously deeply affected by the memory and unable to carry on. After a few moments, he recovered his composure and was able to continue.

'So, as I said, it stands ter reason. Whatever attacked them was lookin' fer somethin'. Somethin' as the lads managed to 'ide away before it came.'

There was another round of animated discussion between the Albard at this suggestion. Trench spoke as it began to subside.

'That's more'n likely what 'appened, Case,' he mused, stroking his chin. 'More'n likely!'

Case looked at Marcus and then at the sphere.

'So!' he spoke gently. 'We may well have something important here – something that whatever attacked the Albard had lost and wanted back. Badly enough to do what it did . . .' Case frowned, leaving the sentence unfinished. He turned away from the table, hands clasped behind him and deep in thought. 'It's a theory, anyway,' he muttered.

During the long silence that followed, Marcus had been thinking hard. There was something about the sphere. Just the way it looked. His mind wandered back to a warm June day at the school's summer fair when he'd been taking a break from running the penalty competition. Walking between the stalls, he found himself in front of a blue and white striped tent with a big sign – 'Madame Zozo' – colourfully chalked on a blackboard and

49

easel perched outside. Looking around to make sure no-one was watching, he peeked through the tent flap and saw a woman, wearing a red and white spotted headscarf and huge gold earrings, engaged in an earnest sounding conversation between herself and a lady wearing a pink frock. They were both peering intently into a bright glass ball, with apparently only Madame Zozo able to see into its swirling depths. Marcus was suddenly back in the room and interrupting the buzz of conversation.

'Case – do you think it could be one of those things a fortune-teller uses. You know, what do they call it? A – a crystal ball?' he blurted.

'A *what*?' he asked. Please explain.'

Marcus felt rather silly.

'Er – well – I'm not sure, really,' he answered. 'It was just an idea. You're supposed to be able to see into the future in one – I think!'

'That would indeed be a valuable thing!' smiled Case.

One of the Albard, however, leaned forward to take a closer look at the black sphere. It was Emdren who spoke.

'I've 'eard of such fings, from the Brendel,' he said, slowly. 'Never guessed I'd see one fer mesself, though!'

'How does it work?' asked Case.

'Dunno!' replied Emdren. 'No idea!'

'I saw someone using one – once,' put in Marcus. 'But I don't think it was for real, though.'

'Can you show us?' encouraged Case.

Marcus looked around uncertainly. He rubbed his hands down his sides before sitting himself self-consciously before the sphere.

'The lady I saw did something like this,' he said, and began to move his hands above it, like a magician about to perform a trick.

Nothing happened and Marcus began to feel foolish again.

'I'm sorry . . .' he muttered apologetically.

He let his fingertips rest gently on its dull surface. It felt strangely warm to his touch. Without being able to say exactly when it started, Marcus began to feel a faint tingling sensation. His fingers seemed to be drawing an elusive energy from the sphere, which now began to throb and surge with increasing intensity. Marcus pulled his hands away, sitting back with a jolt.

'What is it?' asked Case.

'I thought I felt something,' he said, looking up. 'A sort of vibration.'

'Try again!' pressed Case, leaning closer.

Doubtfully, Marcus rubbed his hands on his shirt and looked hard at the sphere. He could see nothing different about it. Gathering courage in anticipation of what he had felt might be coming, he reached out and grasped it firmly in both hands.

The effect was staggering, both on Marcus and the wide-eyed, startled onlookers.

The slight tingle he had felt on first contact with the sphere rapidly intensified into a series of nerve shattering detonations. His body twitched in a series of convulsions as the shockwaves washed through him, until they gradually subsided into an oscillating, almost electrical hum. The sphere had come alive in his hands, emitting a pulsating white glow which gradually spread up through his hands and arms until his whole body was radiant with it. His initial shock gave way to a feeling of well-being, and if he had been afraid at first, he wasn't any more.

Case reached towards him in alarm, but Marcus stopped him, without turning.

51

'Don't touch!' he cried, sensing that Case would be harmed if he did. His voice sounded hollow and distant.

'What's happening, Marcus?' rasped Case, his voice hoarse with anxiety. 'Are you alright?'

'Yes – don't worry,' he answered. 'Look! Something's happening!

'The black sphere began to show a series of cracks which rapidly

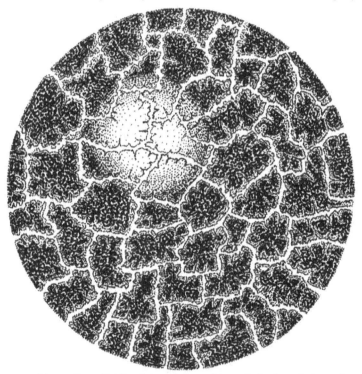

covered its surface, dividing it into dozens of irregularly shaped plates. One by one, each plate was eaten into by an intense orange glow, until, like embers falling back into a fire, they were all consumed. Now a cool, bluish whiteness began to spread from its centre, until Marcus found himself peering into a vast, crystal clear emptiness. As he stared, something began to grow from its depths, slowly at first but becoming rapidly larger and approaching at great speed. Moments later, a face appeared – a face distorted by the convexity of the sphere.

Instinctively, Marcus started backwards as the face filled the globe completely, moving its head from side to side as if trying to get a better look. Glittering eyes took it in turns to fill the sphere, seeming to try to stare beyond Marcus. Finally, the face moved back a little and a pair of piercing grey eyes settled upon him.

'And just who might *you* be?' the face asked, stabbing a long, gnarled and accusing finger at him.

Chapter 4 - Ben

Marcus stared at the apparition before him, taking in the forbidding detail of the face that was staring irritably at him. Long, straggling hair sprouted from the sided of its otherwise bald head. Its slightly yellowing skin was wreathed in wrinkles and heavily lined. It had no eyebrows to speak of, watery grey eyes and a long straight nose whose nostrils seemed to be the source of thin strands of twisted grey and white hair that formed an oriental looking moustache around its puckered lips.

'Well?' grated the voice. 'Lost your tongue?'

Marcus had indeed. He wanted to look at Case for a bit of support, but found himself quite unable to take his eyes from the sharp, compelling image before him. He swallowed hard.

'M-M-Marcus,' he stuttered in a half-whisper. 'My n-name's Marcus.'

'Marcus? Don't recall the name. Identity array and sector location code,' the voice snapped. 'Come on – I haven't got all day!'

'I . . . er . . . I'm sorry . . . I don't know what you mean,' managed

Marcus, completely bewildered.

The eyes closed for a moment in an exaggerated, long suffering gesture. When they re-opened, they looked cross.

'Come along, Guardian. You know the procedures as well as I do, so stop messing about and get on with it!'

'Guardian?' repeated Marcus. 'I have no idea what you mean . . .'

A look of doubt crossed the wrinkled face, nose wiggling suspiciously as it looked closer.

'Is this another of your feeble jokes, Hagman? If it is, I'll . . .'

'Oh, no! This is not a joke,' blurted Marcus. 'More like an accident, I think – or a – a mistake.'

'You drag me halfway across the very stars themselves – accidentally!' stormed the spectre. 'A *mistake*!' it howled, turning away, as if sharing the outrage of it all with some invisible presence nearby.

'Explain yourself and be quick about it!' it ordered, holding up a bony finger.

'I'm sorry to have caused trouble,' began Marcus. 'I didn't mean any harm.'

'Never mind that!' snapped the voice. 'I just want to know what's going on!'

'Well, sir,' began Marcus, trying to be respectful and polite, 'when I picked up the sphere, I didn't know this was going to happen.'

An eye came closer.

'What did you say your name was again?'

The face seemed to be rather less cross and a bit more thoughtful. Encouraged, Marcus continued.

'Marcus, sir.'

'Hmm. So, you found it, did you?'

'No, not me sir – the Albard.'

'The Albard?' it repeated. The eye came closer again. 'Is that them, standing around you?'

'Y-You can see them?' whispered Marcus. It was something of a surprise that the face could look beyond him and into the room.

'Not as well as I would like. Funny looking lot, aren't they!'

Marcus shifted uncomfortably.

'And who's that?' asked the face, pointing past Marcus' shoulder. 'The big skinny one over there.'

'That's Case.' he replied, biting his lip and thinking the face was being unnecessarily rude.

'All friends of yours?'

'Yes!'

The face continued to peer out for a while, before continuing.

'Good! Can't be too careful, these days. And just where did they find it?'

'In the mountains, not too far from here,' Marcus answered, feeling more confident.

'And just where is 'here'?' came another question.

'Stonefort.' he replied.

'Stonefort? Never heard of it. Wait a moment. Stonefort. S-t-o-n-e-f-o-r-t. No! Thought as much. No such place!' The face appeared to have been looking something up.

The eye came closer again.

'Are you sure that's not you, Hagman?' asked the face, examining Marcus closely. 'No – too ugly, even for Hagman!' it cackled, seeming to enjoy its own wit.

'I'm not ugly!' bristled Marcus. 'And I think you're being very rude to my friends, too!'

'Temper, temper!' wheezed the face.

'And Stonefort definitely exists. It's here, all around me.'

Once more the face looked closely, eyes roving. 'I'll look again,' it said. Shortly, and looking satisfied, it spoke again. 'Definitely no Stonefort in my register – nothing even like it. Here – see for yourself!'

Marcus watched as the pages of a large volume filled the sphere. He saw lists of names, all in alphabetical order, but the book disappeared before he had a chance to find Stonefort. He thought for a moment.

'What is that book?' he asked.

'Register of Worlds,' answered the face.

'Then of course it doesn't have Stonefort in it,' cried Marcus. 'Stonefort is a place, here on Galidian! This world is called Galidian!' he repeated.

'No need to shout! I'm not deaf. Let me see, G-a-l-y-'

'With an i,' corrected Marcus.

'Yes, yes,' muttered the face, crossly.

'Yes, here it is. Galidian. Reference dAJ156/472. Hmmm. Haven't heard from there for a long time.'

Marcus heard the book being snapped shut. The face looked hard at him.

'Where's Marchman?' it demanded.

'Who?' asked Marcus.

'Don't play games with me!' menaced the face. 'What have you done with him?'

'I – I'm not . . .' he protested, now feeling very flustered.

'We shall soon see about *that*!' was the foreboding response.

The pale blue glow around Marcus started to change, first to orange and then to a bright, burning red. The now fierce looking eyes seemed to grow and lock into his own. He felt an indescribable, searing pain spread through his entire body until it gathered inside his head, where an intolerable pressure began to build. He wanted to clamp his hands around his skull to somehow hold it together, but he was unable to release his grip on the sphere. Instead, he cried out – a long, anguished wail that scared the wits out of Case and the Albard. Abruptly, and just when Marcus thought he could bear it no longer, the redness left and the pain fell away. He was left sweating, breathless, dizzy and very, very frightened.

The face was dramatically changed, appearing both puzzled and full of concern.

'I don't understand,' it began. 'It seems I was quite wrong – you *are* telling the truth! Please accept my sincere apologies – but I had to make sure. I owe you an explanation!'

A relieved and slowly recovering Marcus waited.

'I am Benderman, Steward of the Guardians. Most call me Ben.'

'Who are the Guardians?' asked Marcus weakly, still shocked by what he had just gone through.

'Between us, we watch over all worlds. Each Guardian carries a Sphere of Light, just like the one you are holding . . .'

'A what?' put in Marcus, now feeling more alert and breathing more easily.

'A Sphere of Light,' came the reply. 'It is one of the greatest sources of power in the universe – but only in the hands of a Guardian. What I don't understand is how *you* are able to use it. What did you do?'

'I just put my hands around it,' said Marcus, simply.

Ben looked at him with growing curiosity. There was a long, thoughtful pause before he spoke again.

'Then you are not from Galidian – if I am not mistaken?' It was a statement of fact, rather than a question.

'Correct!' he replied.

'Let me guess,' smiled Ben, touching a finger to his face. 'You have crossed from Galidian's sister world, Earth. How very, very interesting!'

'But how did you know that?' began Marcus.

'Never mind,' said Ben. 'It is enough to know that you are where you are!'

The smile slowly faded from Ben's face and it became very serious. He leaned forward, speaking earnestly.

'You must listen very carefully to what I have to tell you. The Sphere of Light in your hands belongs to Guardian Marchman. Without it, he is powerless to watch over Galidian, or any of his other worlds for that matter!'

Ben bit his lip before continuing.

'You must find him, Marcus. Find him and return his sphere. Otherwise, I fear the worst!'

'Find him? B – but how? What if I can't? What if – what if something's happened to him?' asked Marcus, trembling with the responsibility just heaped on his shoulders.

'Then it is too late, my friend,' replied Ben, with a deep sadness in his eyes. 'Without Marchman's protection, the evil forces of the Darkness will soon overtake you. And there is no return from its evil clutches – ever!'

'But there must be *something* you can do!' cried Marcus. 'You can't just leave us to . . .'

'It is *you* that must save Galidian, Marcus.' Ben interrupted. 'You and your friends. There is nothing more I can tell you. Do not delay. Find Marchman and guard the sphere with your life until you do. It has *some* power in your hands – that much I can see. But it alone cannot save you. It must be returned to Marchman.'

'Shall I be able to speak with you again?' asked Marcus. Somehow, he knew that time was running out'

'That may be possible, but I am powerless to help you further.'

'Couldn't you send another Guardian?' cried Marcus at the slowly fading Ben. He looked dignified but full of concern.

'I'm sorry. They each have their own work, as indeed, do I. Good luck, Marcus. Find Marchman . . . you must find Marchman . . .'

Ben's voice faded into a whispering echo and Marcus watched as his face finally disappeared.

'No! Don't go . . . please . . . Ben! Come back!' he pleaded, but to no avail.

The blue glow surrounding him gradually flowed back into the sphere, turning orange as it went. Small dark spots appeared on the surface of the sphere, spreading and locking together until it finally lay, quite black and lifeless in his hands.

There followed a profound silence around the table. Marcus released his grip on the sphere and sat back. He suddenly felt sick as waves of sheer exhaustion flowed over him. A stifled groan escaped his dry lips as he fell backwards, drowning in blackness.

Chapter 5 - Preparations

Marcus woke to find Case and one of the Albard looking anxiously at him. He tried to sit up, but a restraining hand from Case stopped him.

'Stay where you are, Marcus. Emdren here says you need to rest for a while. You've had quite an experience!'

'W – what happened?' asked Marcus uncertainly, still confused and unaware of where he was. His head ached something awful.

'Don't you remember?'

Marcus rubbed his head, as if trying to wipe away the pain.

'Here, young feller. Drink this. It'll make yer feel better!'

It was Emdren, offering him a beaker. Helped by Case, he sat up, took the drink and sipped gratefully. The touch of the cool, tangy liquid felt wonderful to his hot, dry lips. He drank the rest of it down and wiped his mouth on his sleeve.

'Could I have another, please?' he asked.

'Course yer can! Right away.'

Taking the beaker, Emdren disappeared.

Marcus lay back, already feeling much better, only to start up again suddenly as the memory of Ben's face flooded back to him.

'The sphere!' he gasped. 'Where's the sphere?'

'Quite safe, Marcus. Don't worry – it's right here!' Case turned aside, produced the leather bag and opened it for the anxious boy to see.

Relieved, he lay back once more and closed his eyes. He felt Case's hand on his head, gently brushing back his hair. He began to drift off, falling comfortably and peacefully back to sleep.

When Emdren returned with a fresh drink for his patient, Case put a finger to his lips.

'He's fine.' whispered Case. 'Fast asleep.'

Emdren nodded, smiling. He put the beaker on the chair by the bed and felt Marcus' brow.

'Fever's almost gone,' he murmured. 'Be right as rain in no time!'

The pair left quietly, being careful not to disturb him. As they did so, General slipped into the room. He decided he could watch over him better from inside. Besides, he didn't want his young friend to wake up alone, not after what he'd just been through.

*   *   *

Marcus stirred and General was at his side in an instant. Moments later, his eyes flickered open.

'Mornin'!' beamed General. 'An' about time, too! How's yer feelin'?'

'Fine, thank you,' he replied, pushing up on his elbows. 'How long have I been asleep?'

'Best part o' two days, I reckon.'

'Two days!' cried Marcus, sitting bolt upright. 'Are you sure?'

'Well, let's see now.'

General began counting off on his fingers. 'There was lunch the day afore yesserday. Dumplins! Luverly they were. An' a roast in the evenin'. Then it was breakfast – pancakes, I fink Grobwold called 'em. Never 'ad 'em before, but they were delishuss. Then fer lunch we 'ad . . .'

'Oh General – you and your stomach!' Marcus laughed.

Not understanding what was causing his amusement, General continued his meal count, which only made matters worse. The more he went on, the louder and more uncontrollable Marcus' laughter became. Slowly, General began to realise that it was his constant references to food that the boy found so funny.

Marcus managed to stop for a moment. He put on his best serious face but could not conceal the playful gleam in his eye.

'And what time is it now?' he asked, as steadily as he could.

'Time fer breakfast!' retorted General, and the two of them burst into helpless laughter and were still falling about when the door opened. In walked Case and Emdren, their faces wreathed in smiles as they caught the infectious merriment, even though they were completely unaware of its cause.

'Well, I can see you're better!' chuckled Case, rather mystified. 'What's the joke?'

'Oh, nothing!' gasped Marcus, his chest heaving.

'Time for breakfast, then!' he announced.

Marcus and General looked at each other, before collapsing together on the bed, literally crying with laughter.

'Well, they say it's the best medicine!' smiled Emdren, equally baffled. 'Best leave 'em to it!'

Twenty minutes later, Marcus and General walked, still grinning, into the kitchen. There were cheery greetings all round. Grobwold in particular, expressed great concern over Marcus' wellbeing and could not do enough for him. Ensuring he was seated well away from General, he carried on serving breakfast. Marcus ate hungrily, grateful to fill the gnawing emptiness resulting from the legacy of two days in bed. The Albard were chattering excitedly with one another, occasionally throwing the odd question at Case. As he ate, he could see that one, or was it two, of the Albard were missing. He counted them. Six. There had been eight. As his plate emptied, his mind gradually tuned in more and more to the buzz of conversation. There was talk of 'supplies' and 'routes' and the like. He realised that they had not been idle during his recovery. Far from it. Nor did he have long to wait before he learned the purpose of their activity.

When everyone had finished eating and Grobwold had cleared away the empty plates from the table, Case began to speak, looking directly across the table at Marcus. He looked fresh and there was colour in his cheeks. Marcus guessed that he'd found time to catch up on some lost sleep.

'So, Marcus. Are you feeling well enough to travel?' he asked.

'To find Marchman?' he returned.

Case nodded.

'Ready!' confirmed Marcus, with determination. He was prickling with excitement as goose pimples rose on his skin.

The Albard greeted his response with enthusiastic approval and banged their mugs on the table – much to the annoyance of Grobwold, who sidled over and removed them, one by one, to the sink.

'Good!' said Case, still looking at Marcus. 'Then provided all goes well in Middlemere, we leave tomorrow!'

A silence descended around the table. Grobwold stopped rattling things and stood quietly as Case continued.

'Provisions and equipment for our journey are being gathered together as we speak, by Hodun and Teshtal. The plan is to make our way back to the place where the Albard found the sphere.'

Case had already noted with satisfaction that Marcus had carried it into breakfast with him.

'We may have a few stops to make on the way, but it seems good sense to start there – to see if we can find any clues that might lead us to Marchman. What do you think, Marcus?'

'Fine!' he replied. 'I can't wait to get started.'

'That's settled, then.' smiled Case. 'First thing in the morning!'

Marcus excused himself from the table and went over to Grobwold. He smiled up at him.

'Are you coming with us, Grobwold?' he asked.

'Nooo, young Marcus,' sighed the Wampy. 'I'm too fat and slow for a journey like that. No – I'll best use the time you're away to give this place a really good clean. There won't be much else to do while you're all gone!'

'I'm sorry, Grobwold. I shall miss you. And thank you for another lovely breakfast!'

'Don't mention it, dear boy!' Grobwold murmured. He had become vague and distracted, as if thinking hard about something.

Case was now standing, trying to catch Marcus' attention from the table. He signalled that he was going to his chambers and that he would like Marcus to join him there, when he was ready. A few minutes later and comfortably seated, Case gave him a searching look.

'You gave us all such a fright, Marcus. Are you sure you're feeling strong enough? It's going to be a long and difficult journey.'

'I'm fine, really,' he answered with a reassuring smile.

'The contact you made with Ben – through the sphere – took a great deal out of you . . . perhaps more than you realise. We thought we'd lost you altogether, at first. Fortunately, Emdren is something of a healer. He managed to bring down your fever and keep you cool. Even so, it was touch and go for the first few hours!'

'One thing is very clear,' Case continued. 'You must not use the sphere again. It seemed to drain the very life force from you. Perhaps Ben knew that towards the end and shut it down in time. Anyway, we don't want you putting yourself at risk again – will you promise?'

Marcus could see that Case meant every word. But he felt perfectly normal right now and couldn't imagine things had been as bad as all that. There again, he had no recollection of being ill, and decided to do as Case had asked – at least, for the time being.

'I promise,' he said. 'But remember what Ben said – that it does have some power in my hands. There might come a time when we'll have to use it again.'

Case looked thoughtful.

'Maybe. But the price for using it may be too high to pay! Perhaps we should decide together, if such a situation arises? Agreed?'

'Agreed!' nodded Marcus.

'Good! Now I'd like to go over a few things with you. Come over to the table and I'll show you on the map.'

For the next half-an-hour or so, Case traced out a probable route, south from Middlemere, across the plains and into the forest. Once there, they would follow a south-westerly track in an attempt to locate the Brendel. He reminded Marcus that the Brendel possessed many powers and might well be able to help them in their search for Marchman. Then, after crossing the river, Case showed how they might skirt the edge of the Southern Wastes to the Albard Caves, and from there to the mountain slopes to where the Albard group had been massacred and the sphere found.

'How long do you think it will take us, Case?' asked Marcus.

'Difficult to say. We shall not be travelling light, as the Albard did when they came here. Also, their route was more straightforward, avoiding the forest. We don't know how long it will take us to find the Brendel – or, more likely, for them to find us. It could take us weeks, rather than days, to reach the Curtains. And who knows where our search will take us after that!'

The pair were interrupted by a knock at the door. It was Grobwold.

'I hope I'm not disturbing you,' he began, shuffling awkwardly towards them, 'but I've been doing some thinking . . .'

'Go on,' encouraged Case. 'What is it?'

'Well, Galidian is my world too. And whatever the danger is that threatens us, I'd like to help!'

Grobwold fidgeted, looking down towards his feet, which he could not see for the overhanging bulk of his middle.

'It will be a long and difficult journey . . .' began Case, patiently.

But Grobwold had the bit between his teeth.

'Yes, I know,' he returned. 'But I'm very strong – and besides, you will all need to eat. Something I can take care of. Besides, I just couldn't bear the thought of everyone out there, somewhere, facing all kinds of terrible danger and me alone here, wondering what's happening.'

Case looked from Grobwold to Marcus and back again.

'It seems to me you've made up your mind,' he smiled. 'Welcome to the Search!'

Grobwold looked delighted and winked at Marcus.

'I won't let you down,' he beamed. 'You'll see!'

With that, and nodding his thanks, he waddled out.

*　　　*　　　*

Later that afternoon, Case took Marcus to the entrance to Stonefort. They wound their way steadily downwards through smooth tunnels and passageways for what seemed an age, while Case explained how it had been built. Originally, the caverns and spiralling tunnels had been formed by an underground river that had dried up, or became diverted, long ago. When Case's ancestors had first explored them, they saw the possibilities and set about constructing Stonefort. Strong walls were built inside large caverns high up in the cliff and divided into several floors, each filled with rooms connected by stairways and passages. The terrace beyond Case's chambers had been chiselled out of the rock in order to provide Stonefort with an unrivalled view of Galidian. Access from ground level had been made easier over the years by constructing steps in some of the steeper tunnels. It was down them that Case and Marcus finally made it to the gate, which was open to the warm afternoon sunshine. As they stepped out from the shadows, Marcus saw a flat wooden bridge, extending from the gate across a narrow but deep ravine, to firm ground on the other side. Strong chains led from slits in the walls above and behind Marcus to the ends of the bridge.

'Should we ever need to,' indicated Case, pointing, 'we can pull up the bridge to cover the gate. Any unwelcome visitor would find it very difficult to get in – not the least because of this.'

He nodded downwards from the low railing that ran along both edges of the bridge. Marcus looked over the edge and whistled. It went deeper than he could see, with sheer walls all the way down. Once the bridge was drawn up, there was clearly no way in. They continued across the bridge and walked for a few minutes towards the lake. A fresh breeze had sprung up and was gently playing back and forth along its surface, leaving rippling trails wherever it went.

'Look, Marcus!' Case had stopped and was looking back at Stonefort.

High above their heads, Marcus could see the balcony cut into the cliff, and a series of small dark rectangles dotted here and there that he knew were windows. He wondered which one was his.

Case was suddenly alert, holding his head in such a way as to catch the slightest of sounds. His keen eyes scanned the slopes down to the south east, in the direction of Middlemere. A moment later, he relaxed.

'It's Hodun and Teshtal,' he told Marcus. 'Let's go and meet them!'

Marcus had heard nothing and could see nothing, even when Case pointed.

'Here, try now!'

Case's strong but gentle grip lifted him effortlessly until Marcus was high enough to make out two tiny figures, bent against the slope, making their way to the gate. He would never have recognised them as two Albard, let alone Hodun and Teshtal.

'Come on!' urged Case. 'Let's go and surprise them!'

Keeping low, the pair moved on a course that Case calculated would intercept them by a small clump of trees, just after the track wound up around a sharp bend.

Case and Marcus soon reached the track and made for the cover of the trees. Panting slightly with the exertion, or more probably the excitement they felt, they waited to surprise their friends. The minutes ticked by until they began to wonder whether Hodun and Ashtar had already gone through.

Finally, deciding to give up their ambush, they left the cover of the trees and stepped back onto the track. The next moment, Case and Marcus were flat on their backs and being firmly sat upon by two laughing Albard. From their hiding places in the branches above them, Hodun and Teshtal had dropped down, bringing them to the ground as they did so.

'Har! Har!' grinned Teshtal. 'Can't catch us out so easy!'

'As it would appear!' conceded Case, good naturedly. 'And good to know, all things considered.'

'Good ter see yer up an' about again, Marcus!' put in Hodun. 'Hopes we didn't frighten yer too much, like!'

The truth was, Marcus had had a scare, not so much for himself as for the precious Sphere of Light slung behind his shoulder. He was opening its pouch as Hodun was speaking, just to make sure it was still in one piece.

'Not at all,' he smiled, relieved that all was well with the sphere.

The four of them scrambled to their feet, brushing away the dust.

'What news from Middlemere?' asked Case.

'Everyfink's ready – all arranged,' beamed Hodun, looking expectantly between Case and Marcus.

'It's tomorrow!' announced Case, anticipating the Albard's next

71

question.

'Temorrer!' they chorused, arms in the air and dancing a little jig. 'Yippee!'

'Anyone would think they were looking forward to it,' Case confided to Marcus.

Teshtal heard him.

'Anyfink's better than 'anging around 'ere, Case. Jus' glad ter be gettin' on wiv it!'

They made their way back to the gate and, as they climbed the step, each of them was thinking about last minute preparations and how they would pass the time until the morning. One thing was for certain – the Search would begin in earnest.

Chapter 6 - The Search Begins

Marcus was woken by General very early next morning. He washed and dressed as quickly as he could and, collecting the Sphere of Light and the backpack he had filled with spare clothes and a bedroll from the chest before going to bed, he made his way down to the kitchen. It was tidier than he'd seen it, with everything cleared and stowed away, except for a huge pile of bacon sandwiches stacked on the table, where the rest of the party sat, tucking in. He put down his pack by the others stacked by the door and joined them. Exchanging the usual morning greetings, he sat down. The atmosphere was tense with excitement and anticipation. Marcus ate in silence, in keeping with the rest of the company. When breakfast was finished, everyone helped to clear away. When all was tidy and Grobwold had his last look around, they filed out, collecting their packs as they went.

Ten minutes later, the whole group were at the gate. Case unlocked and opened it. The sky was still dark except for a faint tinge of brightness away to the east. It felt cold and Marcus shivered, though perhaps more from the prospect of the adventure ahead than the early morning chill.

Grobwold was busy strapping himself between the shafts of a small cart, neatly packed with kitchen equipment and food supplies. Covering it all was a canvas sheet, secured in position with ropes. As the cart rumbled out onto the drawbridge, the rest of the party followed, pausing on the other side until Case had made sure that the bridge had been raised and the door

securely locked. Picking their way carefully in the near darkness, the Quest made off towards Middlemere.

It was late afternoon by the time the already tired and perspiring group arrived. The cheery conversation that had sprung up with the dawn had slowed to a trickle by midday and ceased altogether by mid-afternoon. As they trudged into Middlemere, they were greeted with many a curious stare from the men, women and children who lived there, wondering what this mixed band of travellers was all about.

'Who are you?' came a shy voice at Marcus' shoulder. 'Never seen you before!'

'Marcus,' he replied, politely. 'What's your name?'

'Never you mind!' she replied, laughing cheekily and poking out her tongue at the same time.

Marcus thought she didn't seem quite so shy now, as she skipped and danced alongside him.

'Where are you all going, anyway?' she asked, coy once more.

'Expedition!' replied Marcus, importantly.

'What's one of those?' she asked. She had stopped prancing around and was now walking by his side.

Marcus looked at her, taking in her impish, lightly freckled and blue-eyed face. She was smiling.

'Well, it's a special sort of journey,' he answered, smiling back secretively.

'Where to?' she asked, increasingly curious.

'Don't know yet,' he replied.

She laughed again, but more uncertainly this time,

'So, you're going on a journey and you don't know where you're going? Doesn't make sense!' the girl summarised. 'You must know!'

'Can't say,' said Marcus.

'Oh, go on!' she pleaded. 'I'll tell you my name – it's Jade.'

'Can't. It's a secret!'

'That's not fair!' she pouted. 'I told you my name . . .'

'And I told you mine,' he shot back. 'Now we're even!'

Her cheeks flushed as she aimed an angry look at him and stamped her foot.

'Got yerself a girlfrien' then, our Marcus?' grinned General, coming alongside.

It was Marcus' turn to flush and he looked crossly at General.

'Of course not!' he retorted hotly. 'She's just being nosey, that's all.'

'I am *not*, so there!' Anyway, I think you're a beast and I shan't speak to you again – ever!' With that, Jade spun around and walked away with her nose in the air.

'Dearie me!' teased General. 'Er's upset an' no mistake!

Marcus ignored him. He was watching where the girl had gone and could see her following the progress of the procession as it made its way into the centre of Middlemere, ducking behind trees and buildings from time to time. He smiled to himself again. There was something he liked about that cheeky kid, he decided.

All thoughts of Jade were soon pushed out of his mind when Case stopped outside a large wooden building and took off his pack. As he went in, he was joined by Hodun and Teshtal, while Marcus, the rest of the Albard and a very tired looking Grobwold waited outside, glad of the break.

A few minutes later, Case came out.

'The rest of our supplies are all here, in a shed at the back. The landlord will give us food and shelter for the night, so make the most of it – it'll be the last roof over our heads for some time to come!'

They were shown to a large, fresh smelling barn next to the shed containing the supplies arranged by Hodun and Teshtal. They dumped their things before returning to the inn for their well-earned evening meal. With it, the Albard consumed large quantities of ale and became quite noisy, before Case suggested an early night in preparation for the next day's march. It was a tired but contented lot that settled on comfortable straw beds at the end of their first day on the road. Grobwold snored, but everyone else was too tired to be in the least bit disturbed by it.

*   *   *

Bright sunshine greeted the early risers, who lay rubbing their stiff limbs resulting from the exertions of the day before. Amid yawns and stretching, they got their things together, breakfasted and readied themselves for the long day ahead.

Two small but strong looking ponies were harnessed side by side to the cart that was laden with supplies and equipment. To one side was strapped a barrel of drinking water. A metal cup was chained to the tap, which clattered and tinkled as they set off.

The day passed without incident. Steady progress was made and that evening, they camped under the stars and enjoyed a meal prepared by Grobwold, who despite his weariness, managed to please everyone yet again. He was first to bed, though, knowing he would have to be first up to get breakfast and make sandwiches for their midday break.

Case estimated that they had come about halfway across the plains that lay between Middlemere and the forest and seemed satisfied with the day's march. The Albard organised a series of watches through the night, taking it in turns to perch on a nearby tumble of rocks, from where they were better able to keep an eye on things.

Early next morning, with barely a sign that anyone had rested there the night, the party moved off southwards, hoping to reach the forest before nightfall.

It was Marcus who found her. Mid-way through the morning, they were passing through a small, lightly wooded hollow. Feeling thirsty, he moved alongside the water barrel, intending to take a drink. Just as he was taking the cup, he heard something, rather like a small animal whimpering with fright. It was coming from inside the wagon. Letting go of the cup, Marcus loosened the rope that secured the canvas cover in place, lifted the corner and looked inside. A pair of terrified eyes stared back, puffy and red with tears that ran down freckled cheeks.

'You!' cried out Marcus. 'What are you doing here?'

Case was the first to appear at his side. He watched grimly as Jade was helped from her cramped hiding place. She stood before the silent band, forlorn and miserable, tears coursing down her face.

It was Grobwold who acted first.

'For goodness sake! Don't just stand there – get the little thing something warm to wear. She's half-perished with cold, the poor dear!'

Grobwold busied himself unpacking a sandwich and a few biscuits for her, which she ate like a wild animal. After a drink and clad in something better suited to keeping out the chill wind that was now blowing, she both looked and felt better.

'I think some sort of explanation is in order,' spoke Case, sternly. 'Don't you?'

'I – I'm sorry,' she stammered. 'I don't know – I just wanted . . .' Jade dissolved into tears once more.

Again, it was Grobwold who came to the rescue.

'Let's leave her alone for a while,' he suggested. 'She's had a bad time, stuck in that cart for nearly a day and a half, freezing cold, hungry and thirsty!'

'What'll we do with her?' asked Marcus.

Case was quick to reply.

'She'll have to come with us as far as the Albard Caves. We've come too far to turn back – we just can't afford to lose the three days it would take to get her back to Middlemere and return here. And there's all the extra supplies we'd get through. We can send her back from there.'

Case had spoken loudly enough for Jade to hear. She had stopped crying but still looked scared half to death.

'We had better press on if we're to reach the shelter of the forest before tonight.' he added, casting an eye up at the sky. 'Looks like a storm brewing.'

Right on cue, the wind picked up, blowing the fallen early autumn leaves all about him as if in confirmation of his prediction.

'Stowaways!' he muttered as he turned away. 'Whatever next?'

With Jade perched on Grobwold's cart, they moved out of the hollow. As they climbed out from its protection, they began to feel the full force of the gale that now battered them head on.

Case became concerned, feeling that they would not be able to reach the sanctuary of the forest before nightfall. They ate lunch on the march to help make up for their slower progress, battling through the shrieking wind as they munched. From time to time, uprooted bushes and pieces of scrub flew past them. And yet, the sun shone throughout the afternoon. There was no trace of a cloud anywhere. This worried Case, for in all his years, he had never experienced a wind such as this in a clear sky. His face bore a frown as he bent against the chill blast.

Tough as they were, the Albard were finding the conditions difficult. Marcus trudged along with them behind Grobwold's cart, grateful for the little protection it offered. The gale was unrelenting. One by one they fell back, unable to maintain the pace set by Case. Soon, they were strung out and vulnerable.

Marcus fought his way alongside Case.

'We have to rest!' he shouted, but his words were lost in the howling wind.

He tugged at Case's sleeve.

'Look!' he shouted again, pointing behind him.

Case could see the straggling line stretched out behind him. Realising what was wrong, he nodded at Marcus and began scanning the wind lashed horizon. He cupped his hands to his face.

'This way!' he yelled, moving off to one side.

The two of them battled forwards until Marcus could see what Case was heading for – an outcrop of grey rock, big enough to afford them some shelter against the storm. A few minutes later, they stepped thankfully out of the raging torment into the cover of the buttress. One by one, the others arrived until they were all there, safe and sound. Five minutes later, the Albard had a good fire going and they were all feeling better for the warmth and rest.

Grobwold soon had hot drinks in everybody's hands and as darkness began to fall, they were enjoying platefuls of nourishing stew. As plates were wiped clean with pieces of bread, Case looked at the girl.

'Are you feeling better, Jade?'

She was, but wasn't saying anything and her wide eyes showed that she was still afraid.

'What made you hide in the cart?' asked Marcus, gently.

'Dunno,' she replied. At least she had spoken.

'Your parents will be worried sick, you know!' he added.

Marcus was thinking about all the times he'd been late home. Once, he had stopped out nearly two hours after promising to be home and found his mother crying, beside herself with worry. He'd never done it again.

'I'm an orphan,' Jade said quietly. 'My parents died in a fire two years ago.'

'Poor dear!' muttered Grobwold.

'I'm sorry,' apologised Marcus. 'I didn't know. Who looks after you, then?'

'The orphanage. They don't care, though. I often stay out a lot – nobody ever says anything.'

Marcus returned to the question he'd asked earlier.

'Why did you hide in the wagon?'

'Dunno – just seemed a good idea – after you told me about your expedition. Thought it would be exciting. Better than being in that place, anyway.'

'And what do you think now?' asked Case.

Jade managed a smile.

'It's alright, I suppose!'

'Well, Jade, you are with us now, like it or not – at least for the next two or three weeks!'

Case explained to her that the purpose of the Search was to find someone. Someone important. He did not expand further. The wind roared and buffeted all around them, but try as it might, it could not touch them and one by one, they dropped off to sleep.

The dawn brought with it a cold, clinging mist but at least the wind had gone. Droplets of water clung to their blankets as they unwrapped themselves. The fire had gone out, so after a cold breakfast of bread and cheese, they set off once more. To stay on course in the mist, the Albard took it in turns to walk ahead and line up with the two behind. Progress was slow, but it was important to make sure they were moving in the right direction. Thankfully, around mid-morning, the mist cleared. With a grunt of satisfaction, Case noted the brilliant green fringe of the forest, dead ahead.

'The forest of the Brendel!' he announced.

As the mist cleared from the still distant mountains beyond the forest, Case saw that they were a little to the south of their intended course and he led them around the edge of the forest until, at just about lunchtime, he found the track he was looking for. After a brief stop for refreshments, the group entered the dense, comforting forest greenery, bidding farewell to the sunshine they were leaving behind.

Chapter 7 - The Brendel

As the group made their way into the forest, Marcus struck up a conversation with Jade who was now feeling strong enough to walk with the others. Her colour had returned and her eyes were alive again. She had become very curious as to what the expedition was all about. Case had actually told her very little and she was full of questions.

'Who are we searching for and why is this person so important?' she asked.

'His name is Marchman. He looks after Galidian.' Marcus replied.

'What's he like?'

'I don't know. I don't think anyone does.'

'Then how do you know he's real?' pressed Jade.

Marcus slowed for a moment, thinking how best to answer.

'Because he's lost something that *is* real,' he said, after a pause.

'What?'

'This!' he whispered, pulling open the flap of his leather bag and showing her the sphere nestling inside.

'Looks like a ball,' Jade remarked. 'Nothing special!'

'It doesn't always look like that,' Marcus pointed out. 'It does things!'

'Like what?' she asked.

'I'm not really sure,' returned Marcus. 'But it has a kind of energy inside that is used by Marchman to help keep Galidian safe. Only *he* has the power to use it properly . . .'

'Go on!' Jade urged.

'Well – I can use it too – a bit. I don't know why.'

'How?' she persisted.

Heads bent together as they followed the others through the forest, Marcus told Jade about how he had seen Ben in the sphere and how he had warned them all about the danger that Galidian was in and the importance of getting the sphere back to Marchman.

'Where did you get it from?' she asked, when Marcus had finished.

'The Albard,' he nodded towards them. 'They found it up in the mountains, not far from where they live.'

He stopped for a moment, trying to decide whether or not to tell her the rest of the story.

'Some of their friends had been killed near where they found it,' he added, finally.

'How awful!' cried Jade. 'Why?'

'No-one's sure,' answered Marcus. 'That's why we're going back to try and find out. We hope to find something that will help us find Marchman. There's nowhere else to start.'

'That all sounds terribly dangerous!' she said, looking worried.

Marcus shrugged.

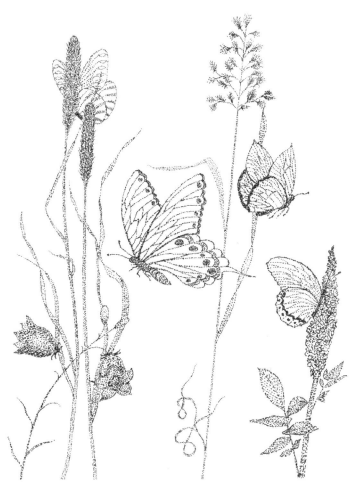

'That's one of the reasons Case wants to send you back to Middlemere – before we go up there!' he told her.

Jade did not answer.

Two or three hours later, the tired and hungry travellers came to a clearing in the forest. Evening birdsong was all around them as they set up camp for the night. The last of the season's butterflies danced in and out of the sunbeams that filtered through the surrounding trees.

Grobwold, who was now getting used to the hardships of the road, was cheerfully humming to himself as he prepared supper. Marcus appeared by his side.

'Hello, Grobwold! Mmm! Smells delicious!' he smiled, looking up.

'Just a little something,' he winked. 'It'll be ready in half-an-hour.'

'Good!' remarked Marcus. 'I'm starving!'

He moved away and found Case. He was sitting against a tree, writing something in a notebook.

'What are you doing?' asked Marcus, plumping himself down beside him'

Case shut the book around his pencil and looked at him.

'It's a diary,' he replied. 'I'm keeping a record of everything that happens. You know, sketch maps of the route we're taking, where we've stayed overnight – that sort of thing. You never know when stuff like that might come in use.'

'May I see?' asked Marcus.

'Here,' said Case, giving him the notebook.

Marcus flicked through the pages and saw blocks of writing, neatly drawn maps and, here and there, little drawings.

'It's lovely!' he murmured after a while. He particularly admired the small sketches. 'You're very clever, Case,' he added, handing it back.

Case smiled.

'Just something to do,' he remarked casually. 'When's food ready?'

'Soon!' replied Marcus. 'Case – tell me about the Brendel. You made them sound very strange when you first mentioned them. Something about them being frightening to look at, but quite friendly when you get to know them. Is that right?'

'The Brendel keep themselves to themselves, Marcus,' he began. 'And yes, they come as quite a shock when you first meet them. They are not like us at all. But you'll see for yourself soon enough. The really interesting thing about them is their minds. You see, Marcus, they do not speak – or at least, I've never heard one. And yet they do – thought to thought – if you know what I mean . . .'

'Like telepathy?' ventured Marcus.

'Yes,' replied Case. 'They also seem to know what you're thinking – what sort of person you are. And if they don't like what they feel about you, they'll just go.'

'But you know them quite well, don't you?' he asked.

Case smiled.

'Yes. They have taught me a great deal over the years – as I've already told you. They are old and valued friends.'

'Do they know that we are here?'

'You can be sure of that, Marcus! But we have a way to travel yet, before they'll show themselves. They like the security of their forest homes and rarely move outside all but the very deepest parts of it.'

'How long before we meet them?'

'Late tomorrow, we have a river crossing to make. After that, another day and a half before we cross it again. Then we can expect them.'

Their conversation was interrupted by Grobwold announcing that supper was ready. Case and Marcus rose to their feet and made their way across the clearing with everyone else. There was a pleasant and relaxed atmosphere, with everyone happy with the progress they had made and the memory of the struggle against the storm the previous day quite put behind them.

They slept well that night, their fourth since leaving Stonefort. As he lay on his back, trying to glimpse the stars as they shimmered through the canopy above him, Marcus reflected that he was pleased Case was keeping a journal. He was already finding it difficult to put everything that had happened so far in sequence. Rolling himself tightly into his blanket, precious bag clutched to his middle, Marcus fell asleep.

It was pitch dark when he woke. Something had disturbed him, but had no idea what. The dying embers of the fire glowed faintly in the middle of the clearing. Sitting up, he strained his eyes and ears, but saw and heard nothing. After a few moments, he pulled his blanket around him again and tried to get back to sleep. He lay there, turning occasionally, trying to get comfortable again. It was no use. Finally, he pulled the blanket over his head against the night. It was then he noticed it. A wispy green light, almost imperceptible. He rubbed his eyes and looked again. It was still there and coming from his bag. Slowly, he lifted the flap. The glow was quite definite now, but still faint. Even as he watched, the glow began to fade until the sphere was dark once more.

From then on, Marcus only slept in fits and starts. He checked the sphere regularly but saw no more of the green glow. When dawn finally arrived, he felt tired and unrested.

At breakfast, he told Case what he had seen during the night. He called the Albard together and they decided there and then that the forest might not be as safe as they had thought. From that moment on, sentries would be posted.

*　　*　　*

That day, the marchers were alert as they strode along the forest track, climbing gently up through the forest tangle on both sides. On their guard because of what Marcus had reported, they looked left, right and upwards as they moved steadily along, peering into the dense undergrowth.

By lunchtime, their mood had lightened somewhat, having neither seen nor heard anything out of the ordinary. The going became easier, for the track was now slightly downhill. As the afternoon wore on, Case's face became more and more serious. He stopped more and more often to look and listen. His mood infected the rest of the party and it was in near silence that they moved further and further in the deepening forest.

Towards evening, Case halted once more. He gestured for everyone to be still and appeared to be listening intently.

'The river!' he announced. 'Not far, now!'

Sure enough, a few minutes later, the expedition found itself by the banks of a wide, sluggish river. The track led directly into it. The tall, creeper filled trees on both sides of the river leaned inwards, their upper branches coming together so there was little sky to be seen.

'We'll cross now!' decided Case, after looking up and down the stretch of river. 'There's a good place to camp on the other side.'

Taking a length of rope from the back of the wagon, he tied one end to a convenient tree and waded across to the opposite bank. Having secured the lifeline, he signalled for the party to cross. The cart was first across, with Richmane coaxing the reluctant ponies. Jade and Marcus sat up there with him, enjoying the ride. Next came Grobwold, easily moving through the current until, with a helpful hand from Jade and Marcus, he and his cart arrived safe and sound on the other side. The rest of the Albard, except for Welgar, came splashing across, pulling themselves along the rope. Finally, Welgar undid the rope from the tree and secured it around his waist. He waded across, not without some difficulty, until he was pulled safely to the bank. The whole crossing had taken less than half an hour. Twenty minutes later, those who had got wet during the crossing were drying themselves by a good fire at the camping place Case had told them about earlier.

The night passed without incident. The sentries had reported nothing. Marcus slept like a log, waking refreshed and ready for another day's slog through the forest. It was hard going, too, for the track was quite steep in places. It was much narrower and tree roots intruded upon it, making it difficult for the carts to negotiate. Both needed a frequent helping push to keep them moving.

From time to time, Marcus took a peek at the sphere, but each time it lay there quite unchanged from its familiar dull blackness.

Another night passed without incident and halfway through the next day, they found and forded the river again. It had been almost a week of constant travel, so everyone took the opportunity stay at the riverside long enough to wash both themselves and their clothes. The trees here were thinner and some large, flat rocks nearby served as drying stones for their clothes, warmed by the midday sun as they were. If Marcus had taken a look just then, he would have seen the sphere gradually take on the green glow he'd seen on his first night in the forest. He might also have seen a small, beady pair of eyes watching from the cover of the dense vegetation that smothered the gaps between the trees. But he did not. The leaves closed silently over and the eyes retreated, glinting with satisfaction as they went.

When the companions were dressed, ready to move on and feeling much refreshed, Marcus looked at Case. He was looking concerned.

'Something wrong?' he asked.

'I'm not sure. I expected the Brendel to be here – or at least one or two of them. But there's no sign . . .'

The forest was quiet, unnaturally so.

After a long stare all around him, Case moved off with Marcus at his side. The Albard followed, with the carts bringing up the rear and Jade chattering away with Grobwold. Case became more and more fractious as they pressed on, battling the steady incline as the forest worked its way towards the lower slopes of the Curtains that lay beyond.

The evening light was beginning to fade when Case stopped abruptly.

'They aren't here!' he stated.

'How do you know?' asked Marcus. He was also beginning to feel worried, his voice sounding small and lost in that darkening wilderness.

'I can sense them. Feel their presence. They're not here.'

Case set his jaw determinedly and pushed on. He seemed possessed and it was only with much pleading that he was persuaded to call a halt for the night, which had all but closed in on them. The alarm they all now felt prevented them from building a fire and they sat huddled together for warmth and comfort in a small clearing, just to one side of the track. Moonlight filtered eerily through the treetops, casting strange and fearful shadows all around them. To make matters worse, the sphere began to glow intermittently, waxing and waning as if some invisible presence was coming and going. No-one slept much until the dawn began to creep back into the sky, when weariness and exhaustion caused them all to drop off, one by one.

When Marcus opened his eyes, it was already mid-morning. He sat up and immediately noticed that Case was missing. On his blanket lay his diary, pencil to one side. A page had been torn out, bearing a scribbled message. Quickly, Marcus crawled across to it, disturbing the still sleeping Albard as he did so. By the time he reached it, they had begun to wake, grumbling. He picked up the note and read 'Gone to find the Brendel – back soon.'

*　　　*　　　*

After writing the note and leaving it where he knew it would be found, Case left the clearing as quietly as he could and back onto the track. All the time, his eyes searched the canopy overhead for signs of the Brendel. By now, he was certain that something had happened. They were nowhere around. Where were they? What had happened to cause them to leave? His head was full of questions and wild imaginings as he approached that part of the forest where he had met with them many times before.

There was a strange, deathlike stillness all around him as Case faltered in his stride and stepped instinctively to one side of the track, ready to duck under cover. He sensed something, not far ahead. When he was satisfied it was not on the move, he glided noiselessly from tree to tree, watching and listening as he went. Suddenly, a low and agonised moan entered his head. He knew instantly it was one of the Brendel. Forcing the possible reasons for that sinister cry out of his mind, Case concentrated as

92

he had never done before.

'Where are you, my friend? Tell me where you are!' he thought as hard as he could. 'I can't see you!'

From somewhere beyond him, Case received a weak and feeble reply.

'Is – that – you – Case?'

'Yes, Ringer, my friend. Where are you?'

Case recognised the mind of Ringer, the Brendel who had perhaps taught him the most. Almost mad with anxiety, he broke into a steady run, to more quickly find his stricken friend. As he stumbled into the clearing where Brendel homes were woven into the branches high above, he slowed involuntarily to a teetering stop, like some run-down clockwork toy. His face was already a mask of horror and tears filled his disbelieving eyes.

He fell to his knees, legs too weak to support him any longer. He forced himself to look around. Everywhere were Brendel bodies. Men, women and children, hanging grotesquely from trees, pinned with great, crude stakes and lying on the ground in shapeless heaps. Worse still, they had been mutilated, with limbs and heads missing. Kneeling on all fours, Case threw back his head and let out a long, blood curdling howl of anguish, lasting a full ten seconds, before falling, sobbing on the blood-stained glass.

'Above you, Case. Here!'

Case sprang to his feet and looked up, wiping the tears from his eyes. High above him, hanging in the branches, was Ringer.

'Oh, my dear friend! What evil has been done here?' Case thought at him, a fierce anger filling his heart. 'Hold on, Ringer. I'll be with you in a moment!'

Case quickly scaled the tree and was soon moving out along the branch that was supporting Ringer. As he tried to untangle his friend from the grasping twigs and thorns, he saw that his body was badly bruised and lacerated.

'Ringer, what happened? Who did this to you?' he demanded as he worked to pull the snaring foliage away.

'They threw things, Case.'

'Who did?' he pressed.

'Greblocks, Case . . . forces of darkness!' came the feeble response.

'Greblocks?' returned Case, puzzled. He had never heard of them. 'Never mind. You can tell me about them later. Now I must get you to help – it's not far. I'll try not to hurt you too much. Be brave, my friend!'

With an enormous effort, Ringer closed off the pain from his mind so that Case would not feel it. When the excruciating climb down the tree was over, Ringer begged Case to put him down.

'Burn it, Case! Burn it all, so that no other eye shall witness the terrible thing that has happened here. I have been looking at this for three days now – please burn it!'

'It shall be so!' Case grimaced. A few minutes later, as the forest roared and crackled in a cleansing inferno behind the retreating pair, Case tried to keep his limp burden conscious.

'What happened to the others?' he asked.

'Escaped through the treetops,' Ringer thought back. 'Gone east.'

'How many?' Case continued.

'About fifty. We lost eighteen in the ambush . . .'

'Almost nineteen, my friend,' replied Case, grimly. 'Almost nineteen!'

Twenty minutes later, Case arrived back at the camp and placed Ringer directly into the care of Emdren.

*   *   *

It was with considerable alarm that Marcus and the others watched as Case, carrying something about half his size, came crashing into the clearing. He was calling for Emdren even before he lowered his burden onto his own blanket. Sensing the urgency of the moment, no-one spoke. Emdren was quick to fetch his bag and was soon busy taking out ointments and bandages, while a heavily breathing Case looked on. Despite his exertions, he was looking pale and drawn.

'What's happened, Case?' whispered Marcus.

'Terrible things,' he muttered, after a pause. He wiped his sweaty brow on his sleeve.

'Drink this, Case. Make you feel better!'

It was Grobwold and by the troubled expression on his face, he knew that something dreadful had happened.

'Is this . . .?' began Marcus.

'One of the Brendel? Yes, Marcus. His name is Ringer and I fear he's badly hurt. The others have gone, or . . .' Case's voice trailed off as he looked in the direction of what had been the Brendel village.

He never finished the sentence.

Later that afternoon, Ringer died from his wounds. It was a sad and fearful group that gathered around Case after his friend had been buried. He told them what he had seen that morning and how he had found Ringer and brought him down from the tree. As he spoke, there was a steely glint in his eyes that did not sit well with the tears that flowed freely down his face.

'Change of plan!' he muttered through his teeth. 'We have to find what's left of the Brendel. We're going east.'

Chapter 8 - Change of Plan

It was Trench who spoke next. He sounded troubled'

'What about the Albard Caves, Case?'

'What do you mean?'

'Well, we were going there next, remember? But if'n we change plans, there'll be no-one to warn 'em of the danger they're in – right?'

Case thought for a moment.

'Of course, you're right, Trench. What do you suggest?'

'Well, I was thinkin' I should take Hodun wiv me and get 'em out of there. Wiv what we've seen here and that mess on the mountain, the Albard Caves are proberly next in line. What d'yer reckon?'

'How long will it take?' asked Case.

Trench stroked his chin. It was Hodun who butted in, though.

'Two, three days at the most, wiv jus' the two of us.'

'Right!' decided Case. 'We split up, then. Grobwold, could you set aside some provisions for Trench and Hodun?'

Grobwold bustled away, glad to have something to do.

'Trench – where will you take the Albard?' asked Case.

'Dunno. What d'yer fink Hodun?'

Before he could reply, Case made a suggestion.

'Why not take them to Stonefort – it's safe there. There's plenty of room for you all. And on the way back, you could warn the folks in Middlemere of what might be coming. At least that will give them a chance to defend themselves, if need be.'

'Good idea!' nodded Trench. 'That's settled, then. Come on Hodun – let's get going!'

'W – What about me?'

It was Jade who had spoken. Case had forgotten they were supposed to be taking her to the Albard Caves and returning her to Middlemere from there.

He shook his head. 'It's too dangerous, Jade. I can't let you go with these two – and anyway, you'd slow them down.'

Trench and Hodun looked relieved. They did not want the responsibility of having her in tow.

'Then I can stay with you, Marcus and the rest?' she asked, brightening.

'No choice!' returned Case, drily.

*   *   *

Within the hour, they were ready to continue. With light packs on their backs, Trench and Hodun had already bid their farewells and set off back to the river which they would follow until it turned south. From there, they only had a few hours of forest to negotiate before coming to the western edge of the Southern Wastes, about a day or so from the Albard Caves.

Case led them along the track towards what was left of the Brendel Village. Well before reaching it, however, they took a left fork in the track that headed east. The path was good and they made swift progress. Shortly before nightfall, they made camp. Once more, it was fireless, for they did not wish to attract unwanted attention. Supper was eaten in silence, everyone preoccupied with the fate of the Brendel and the memory of Ringer's lonely grave.

After a fitful night, Case was up early. He stood for a long time on the edge of their camp, head on one side. When he joined the others at breakfast, he announced that he had sensed the Brendel some distance to the south east.

All that morning, Marcus, Jade, Grobwold and the six Albard followed him. Sensing his urgency, no-one complained at the pace he set. Shortly before noon, he stopped, head cocked on one side again.

'That's them!' he cried. 'Wait here!'

As Case disappeared into the forest, the rest of the party spread themselves beneath a large tree, glad of the break and munching biscuits handed out by Grobwold. There was ham and cheese to go with them, but the bread had run out.

Some two hours later, just as Marcus was beginning to get worried, Case returned. There were two Brendel with him.

'This is Linden and Hornbeam, and they have agreed to come with us. I have told them all about you, Marcus – and, of course our search for Marchman. It appears they may be able to help!'

Marcus looked at the two Brendel. They seemed altogether different from the crumpled and mortally wounded Ringer, but then, he had never seen him standing. They were very ape-like, with short, heavy bodies and long arms that brushed the ground, even as they stood. But it was their heads that took his attention. Completely hairless, with large, sharply pointed ears and huge, dark brown eyes. There was hardly a nose to speak of and large, half open mouths in which were set the most ferocious looking teeth he had ever seen. Altogether, the stuff of nightmares, Marcus decided.

Over the next few minutes, Case told them all he had learned from the Brendel. They had, as they already knew from the unfortunate Ringer, been attacked without warning by a band of Greblocks – fearsome and well organised savages who swarmed all over them, killing without mercy. Their presence had gone undetected as the Brendel were not able to catch their thoughts, as they could with other creatures. If it had not been for the fact that Greblocks had no facility in climbing trees, the entire village would have perished at their hands. They appeared to be driven by some great force and incapable of individual action, as they cold-bloodedly and systematically butchered those they managed to catch.

Case looked at everyone. He had been saving something – something that he was sure would give them all hope.

'Before the attack,' he began, 'the Brendel had sensed a new presence on Galidian. With their remarkable powers, they detected a kind of mental distress signal from somewhere on the other side of the Curtains – in The Shadowlands. Although they were unable to exactly pinpoint the source of these thoughts, they were certain about one thing – that it came from someone of profound wisdom and good intent. And that the cause of its distress was some kind of great personal loss!'

Case looked around with an excited gleam in his eye.

'Don't you see – it's Marchman! It must be!'

This was important news indeed. Marcus, Jade and Grobwold exchanged glances, nodding at one another.

The reaction of the Albard was not so enthusiastic, however.

It was General who voiced their objection.

'Whoever it might be is on the other side of them there mountains. An' that's no place for the likes of us! You know that as well as we do!'

As usual, Case was thoughtful with his response.

'You're probably right, General. But let's look at the alternatives. It's my guess that these Greblocks, whatever they are, do not belong on Galidian. Nor does the force that controls them. Somehow, Marchman has fallen foul of this evil and has been parted from his power to banish them – his Sphere of Light. So, the choice appears to be to return to Stonefort and wait to be overrun by these creatures, or to try and fight back by finding Marchman – wherever he is!'

The Albard looked at one another. Case's dramatic appeal had struck home and they knew in their hearts that there was no alternative.

'And please don't forget Linden and Hornbeam. It's more than possible that they can lead us right to him!' he pointed out, to add extra weight to his argument.

Their decision was agreed there and then. They would go to The Shadowlands whatever dangers they might have to face. Case looked around.

'With Galidian at stake, I can't think of a better team to win it back. And that goes for you too, young Jade!' he said, smiling.

It was an expectant and thoughtful band that settled down to make fresh plans that afternoon. Case occasionally engaged in silent conversations with the Brendel. Until he had translated their thoughts, the others had no idea what was passing between them. It was very strange for them to witness Case turning from Linden to Hornbeam and back, as if in deep discussion, yet saying nothing.

Between Case, the Brendel and the Albard, they established that it was much too dangerous to travel west, where the Greblocks had already shown their presence. It seemed a reasonable assumption that they were gradually spreading down from the high mountains above the Southern wastes and making their way north, through the forests. While the Brendel were unable to detect their presence, Marcus was! At least, this was the only explanation that anyone could come up with to have caused the intermittent green glow around the sphere. As long as Marcus kept an eye on it, they would have some warning of approaching Greblocks. Clearly, they had been fortunate so far. They now suspected that they had been nearby on several occasions over the past few days – possibly even been seen by them. Perhaps they had been forward scouts, or small advance parties, and therefore not in sufficient numbers to mount an attack.

This led them to suppose that further delay would be dangerous, for the Greblocks clearly knew about them and would be searching for them as they spoke. They decided that the best plan was to try and outrun them, away to the east.

While the Albard were exchanging concerns over the dangers that Trench and Hodun might be exposed to on their journey back to the Albard Caves, and whether they would make it or not, Case was looking hard at the maps of Galidian that he carried in his pouch along with his diary. He showed everyone where they were now, and the route they had taken so far. Between Case, Linden and Hornbeam, they decided that it would be best for the surviving Brendel to get as far to the south east as they could. There was plenty of forest there, and if necessary, they could head for the coast and make for the temporary safety of one of the islands – at least giving them a chance to regroup.

Case re-joined the main party.

'This is what we suggest,' he began. 'It's less than a day's march out of the forest from here. The track will bring us out onto the plains and if we continue east through Flower Vale, we'll be in Marchant in four days from now.'

'How will that help, Case?' asked Marcus. It was clear from the maps that Case was leading them in quite the opposite direction.

'Two things!' he replied. 'First, if we head straight for the Curtains, we would have to risk several more days working our way through unknown forest. Then the mountains themselves. The Curtains are a formidable barrier, high and cold beyond anything we have experienced. There is no guarantee we could find a pass through to The Shadowlands beyond. And who knows what dangers might be lying in wait for us every step of the way.'

He paused.

'Second, by heading for Marchant, we'll be able to provision ourselves again and charter a ship to take us down here . . .'

Case traced his finger down the coastline.

' . . . through or around the Fire Islands, across the Bay of Whales, past The Scapps and into Wrackwater Sound. Then, if we can find a path between the swamps and the mountains, we can work our way into The Shadowlands from the south.'

The Albard appeared to be concerned about this.

'What if we can't find a way through, Case?' asked Teshtal.

'We must, my friend – we must. And if we travel light, we'll have a better chance – even if we have to climb higher into the mountains than we'd like.'

The map was studied and discussed at great length, fingers pointing here and there. Before long, however, it became clear that Case's plan was really their only option.

'That's settled, then,' he said, straightening up. He looked up through the trees as he folded his maps and put them away. 'I reckon we have three or four hours of daylight left and suggest we leave now. We'll be in Flower Vale in a couple of days!'

The camp bustled with activity and was ready for the off in a matter of minutes. Linden and Hornbeam had, in those few minutes, disappeared into the treetops to inform the rest of the Brendel of their plans. As soon as they returned, everyone filed off behind Case, trying hard not to think of what might be coming after them through the forest and concentrating on making as much haste as possible.

Chapter 9 - Voyage South

The Search picked its way through the forest until it was too dark to see any more. They felt reasonably fresh after their long rest in the middle of the day and as the forest began to thin out, the decision was taken to continue as soon as the moon had risen. Snatching what rest they could, they waited, looking anxiously into the darkness. Marcus kept his eye on the sphere throughout the wait, thankfully with nothing to report. As the nearly full autumn moon rose, the travellers gathered their things and trooped off with sufficient light for them to thread their way ever closer to the edge of the forest.

To the welcoming accompaniment of birdsong, dawn broke ahead of them as they emerged, breathing thankful sighs of relief, from the forest and onto the plains. Despite their collective weariness, steady progress was made until Case called a halt, having found a good place to camp for the night. Exhausted though they were, the Albard set up watch. Linden and Hornbeam were fearful of the open spaces all around them and could do little more than huddle together for the night, gaining what comfort they could from one another. Case remained nearby, trying to reassure them with his thoughts until, they too, managed to get some sleep. In the morning, after another cold breakfast, they turned a little more to the south and wound their way all day through grassy, brush covered slopes and into the wide, rolling landscape that marked the beginning of Flower Vale. Finding a small hollow that would protect them from the cold evening breeze that had sprung up, they made camp and enjoyed a hot meal before settling down to their second night under an open sky since leaving the forest. The early morning sunshine saw them break camp and move off down the

gently sloping valley. They had a good view, now they were well into the open, of the towering, snow-capped Curtains to their right. Each realised the folly of attempting to cross them, glad they had followed Case's advice.

Flower Vale was aptly named. It was a riot of yellows and blues and the warming air was full of bees and other flying insects looking for pollen and whatever else they could find. Swallows flitted here and there, taking their fill before flying off to their winter quarters, wherever they might be. High flying larks with their shrill melodies kept them company all day. On

106

and on they marched, alert and watchful throughout the long day. Towards evening, Case stopped and pointed out the sea, just visible on the horizon directly ahead.

'We'll be in Marchant by early afternoon, the day after tomorrow,' he announced with satisfaction.

* * *

And they were. Feeling increasingly safe and secure the further they went, it was an almost chirpy set of travellers that strode into the outskirts of the port. They found lodgings for themselves while Case went off to look for a suitable vessel to carry them south. While he was away, the rest of the party took the opportunity to wash themselves and their grimy clothes. When Case returned that evening, he seemed pleased to have secured the services of a Captain Lugger, the owner of a tidy, two-masted sailing ship called 'Liberty'.

'Perhaps a good omen!' he told them, with twinkling eyes. 'Captain Lugger and his crew have just put in from Eastport on the off-chance, looking for cargo. He's agreed to take us to Wrackwater Sound and wants us on board tomorrow evening!'

The remainder of that day and most of the next was spent trading off the ponies and carts against fresh supplies. Late that afternoon, they hoisted their provisions and equipment aboard the 'Liberty' and sorted out their cabins. They were cramped and in no sense luxurious, but everyone felt at home, especially when Grobwold busied himself in the galley and produced a meal that Captain Lugger and his crew declared the best they had ever eaten. After dinner, the captain announced they would be sailing on the morning tide and could expect a voyage of anything between three or four days and a week, depending on winds and currents. Lulled by the gentle motion of the 'Liberty' at anchor, they all slept soundly.

Awakening to the sound of a bell being rung and the bustling

footsteps of the crew running up and down on the planking above their heads, everyone was keen to go up on deck to watch the 'Liberty' set sail and leave port. From the wharf, a few disinterested dockhands witnessed their departure. Otherwise, they slid out into the open sea unnoticed and without ceremony.

For the first hour, they watched the coastline slide by, becoming less and less distinct as it receded. Captain Lugger sailed due east, before picking up the assistance of a strong current that would carry them towards the Fire Islands, still a considerable distance somewhere below the horizon. One by one, the passengers made their way back down through the hatch and gathered in the galley where, once more, Grobwold had been hard at work. By lunchtime, and feeling refreshed from two weeks of danger, excitement and physical hardship, many of the company were becoming restless. They paced up and down the deck with nothing to do except watch the sea or the ever-distant coastline. Restlessness turned to boredom by evening, but it was not to last for long. The crew were busy taking in sail and lashing down the cargo hatches. Case made his way to the stern of the 'Liberty', where Captain Lugger was steering and watching the sky at the same time.

'Bad weather on the way?' he asked.

'More than likely,' he replied, nodding his bearded and weather-beaten face over his left shoulder towards the eastern horizon. Case looked and saw a single cloud, shaped rather like an upside-down soup dish. It was not fluffy or billowy like those dotted in the sky ahead of them. It seemed to be made up of a series of ringed layers, causing an almost spiral effect.

'Seems harmless enough,' he commented.

'Give it a couple of hours,' grimaced Captain Lugger. 'You'll see!'

How right he was. Within the hour, the wind had picked up considerably and the sea with it. The schooner pitched and tossed in the cross wind that seemed bent on driving them to the shore. With the skills learned from many years of seafaring, Captain Lugger kept the 'Liberty' on course. Another hour after that, any remaining sail had been furled and they were riding a fierce and savage storm. Stinging rain lashed at those who needed to be on deck whilst those below endured the misery of sea-sickness, except for Linden and Hornbeam who seemed quite undisturbed by the pitching and rolling of the vessel. The galley was in complete shambles, with a rather green and forlorn Grobwold wedged into one corner. Captain Lugger and his crew seemed well in control, however, as they went about their business with an almost exaggerated nonchalance, stopping into the galley from time to time to replenish their hot drinks and never appearing to spill a drop.

All night long, the wind and the waves plucked at the 'Liberty'. But she was a strong ship and in good hands. When dawn broke, the gale had all but subsided and by mid-morning, the sea was nothing more than a gentle, rolling swell – which did nothing for the appetites of the miserable passengers, nor for their relish of sea travel! Spirits were soon lifted by the sight of the Fire Islands on the southern horizon, dead ahead. Thin columns of smoke drifted up from the peaks on two or three of the larger islands, evidence of the still active volcanoes that gave the islands their name.

Going up on deck now that the 'Liberty' had steadied herself, Marcus, Case and the others took in lungfuls of fresh air, glad to be away from the nauseous and acrid smells down below – to which they had all involuntarily contributed during the night. After the all-night vigil of himself and his crew, Captain Lugger decided to put into one of the many safe and sheltered anchorages around the Fire Islands that night. By evening, they had thoroughly scrubbed out and cleaned their quarters and

110

by next morning, everyone was quite recovered having benefited from a hot supper and a good night's sleep.

Leaving the shelter of the small inlet, the 'Liberty' was guided between the remaining islands before running into the Bay of Whales. It was aptly named, for the huge creatures were in evidence all around them. It was an unnerving experience, watching these gigantic sea mammals breaking the surface and sending up powerful jets of water from their blowholes. Enormous tails lashed the sea with a ferocity that could be heard above the rigging and protesting timbers that creaked in the fair wind and hurried them south westward across the whales' playground. The captain reassured them that collisions between whales and ships were unheard of, even in these turbulent waters.

Nevertheless, it was with some relief that they left the whales behind later that day. Captain Lugger kept the 'Liberty' close to shore from then on, explaining that he was making for a narrow channel between the mainland and The Scapps, a small collection of islands that they would see, with luck, before sunset. By negotiating this strait, he explained, they would save half a day, enabling them to anchor up for the night and still arrive in Wrackwater Sound at the same time as if they had sailed all the way around The Scapps without stopping.

They dropped anchor safely at the eastern entrance to the channel as dusk descended. They were in a stone's throw of the shore and the 'Liberty' bobbed gently at her mooring as the travellers prepared to spend their last night on board. There was much bustling and bumping in those cabins as they collected their things together by lamplight. Finally, all was ready for the landing they expected to make at around noon the next day.

Grobwold worked wonders in the galley that evening, knowing it

111

would be their last decent meal for some time to come, for not even he, with his great strength, could carry the equipment necessary for even basic cooking.

With the sea air wafting across them from open portholes and full bellies, they slept well, waking refreshed and more than ready to take on the challenges they knew they must face later that day and, in all probability, for some time to come. As Captain Lugger and his crew negotiated the channel, the Search busied themselves with last minute preparations, dividing up the supplies they had collected in Marchant into manageable packs. All was ready when they emerged into Wrackwater Sound. The ocean current swept past it to the south, leaving this stretch of water relatively undisturbed as a result. Being fed by fresh water from a huge river delta and the swamps that lay beyond, the water was rich in plant life – especially a thick, bluish green weed that abounded everywhere. Again, keeping close to the shore, Captain Lugger and his crew were taking great care not to become entangled in it. Finally, he lowered the sails and dropped anchor, saying that this was as far as he could safely take them. A short distance away to starboard lay a small, shallow bay fringed by a sandy beach. Beyond it lay dunes, above which they could see the Curtains, stretching away northward. Between the two lay a misty, uninviting area under which they knew lay a vast swamp. The crew lowered a rowing boat and one by one, the Search climbed down into it, passing their packs ahead of them as they went. They were rowed expertly to the shore, where they unloaded and carried their supplies a little way up the beach. The group watched and waited in silence as their ferry returned to the 'Liberty'. With mixed feelings, they saw it weigh anchor and set sail due south. Later, they knew, it would steer east, before turning north to make its way back up the coast towards Marchant.

Now, as they stood waving their goodbyes to Captain Lugger and his crew, they knew they were completely alone with only their wits and courage to face the challenges and dangers that lay ahead.

Chapter 10 - The Swamps

After watching the 'Liberty' until she was well under way, the Search shouldered their packs and made for some high ground just beyond the dunes. They reached it about half an hour later, by which time they had climbed high enough to stop and take a good look around. Behind them, their ship had become a tiny, white speck out in the sound, almost out of the weed and into open water. Ahead, mountains sloped steeply down into the swamps that stretched away to the west as far as the eye could see. They looked sinister and uninviting, shrouded in mist with just the occasional tree showing through.

Without warning, a series of deep, primeval roars rose into the air followed by a long, drawn out shrill scream. This left the travellers looking at one another, imaginations running riot. Except for Grobwold, who stood gazing out over the marshes with a distant, faraway look in his eyes.

'W – What was that?' whispered Marcus.

Grobwold smiled.

'Nothing to worry about,' he mused. 'Distant cousins of mine, I shouldn't wonder!'

'What do you mean, Grobwold?' asked Marcus, moving closer.

'Oh, it's just that all this reminds me of home,' he answered. 'All a

very long time ago, now. Never could stand all the slime, you know – and the endless moving around! So, I decided to leave. But it's nice to see it all again!'

A disbelieving Jade shuddered. 'You used to live in a place like that?'

'It's not really so bad!' he remarked, before adding 'Not so cosy as Stonefort, though, I must admit.' He smiled down at his two companions, putting his arms around their shoulders reassuringly.

Meanwhile, Linden and Hornbeam had been standing side by side with the sun at their backs. Case was nearby. As the cries from the swamp died down, he came striding back.

'According to the Brendel, we should head north west. But that would take us straight through the swamp. So, we'll try and find a way around, keeping close to the edge and cutting across to the west when we can.'

They moved off, slowly descending to the foot of the slope to where the line of the swamp began. As the afternoon wore on, they made good time, although the flies bothered them a lot. Grobwold showed them how to smear marsh mud on their arms and faces. Unlikely as it seemed, this worked. Marcus and Jade grinned and pulled faces at one another, enjoying the spectacle of themselves. As the sun crossed the sky, the marshland shimmered and occasionally restricted their view as mist swirled in on them from time to time. As evening approached, cool air began to slide down from the mountains to their right and across their path, pushing the mists back into the middle regions of the swamp. All afternoon, they heard strange, intermittent cries and calls and became quite hardened to them.

As they rounded a slight bend, the Search came to a sudden stop. For some time, the slope up to the mountains had become steadily steeper. Now, directly ahead, they saw towering and forbidding cliffs. The swamp began where they finished, offering no path of any description for the party to follow. It was clear that those monumental slabs of vertical rock could not be scaled. Furthermore, they ran upwards into the mountains as far as the eye could see, forming an impassable barrier to their progress.

Their worst fears were realised. They could not go forward or to either side. The only option was to go back the way they had come, away from their objective and with no prospect of finding another route. Anxiously, Case scanned the mountain range for a possible passage through, but stare as he might, he could see nothing that gave him any hope at all.

Bitterly disappointed, they agreed to make camp for the night and decide what to do in the morning. No-one spoke much that evening and it was with grim resignation that they tried to settle down and get what sleep they could, trying to shut out the raucous, nerve shattering cries from the interior of the swamp.

In the shrouded mist of early morning, they were startled awake by an ear-splitting scream. Scared nearly to death, they rose from their blankets as one. A pointing, deathly pale and petrified Jade had seen it first. Hardly daring to turn their eyes in the direction Jade had indicated, they all witnessed the terrifying sight of a piece of the swamp heaving itself in their direction. A huge, shapeless bulk detached itself and came, lurching and writhing towards them in a swaying, hypnotic manner. Still some distance from the horror-stricken watchers, it stopped, swaying slightly.

'It's only me!' it gurgled. 'Sorry if I frightened you!'

The voice was vaguely familiar but the spectre of this ghastly swamp monster held them transfixed and rooted to the spot. Something resembling a huge mouth began to twist and gyrate. A moment later, its head turned to one side as it spat out a huge glob of mud.

'Grobwold? I – is that you?'

It was General who found his voice first, shaky though it was.

117

'Course it is!' came the reply, this time clearly recognisable as Grobwold's voice.

'Fank the twinklin' stars above for that! You 'ad me 'art goin backwards, yer great lummox!' he shouted. 'What d'yer wanna go around frightenin' us like that fer?'

The spell was broken and everyone heaved a collective sigh of relief – except for Linden and Hornbeam, for they had sensed who it was right from the beginning.

'I said I was sorry!' gurgled Grobwold, unabashed. 'Anyway, I bring good news – we can go through the swamp!'

Before General could throw more insults, Case cut him off.

'What do you mean, Grobwold?' he asked, moving towards him.

'Just as I said, Case. We can go through the swamp!'

'But how?' was all he could manage.

'It's like I was saying to these two yesterday,' he continued, nodding towards Marcus and Jade. 'These marshes are like a second home to me – born and brought up in them, you know! Anyway, I took myself off last night to have a good look around. Apart from one or two nasty characters, most of the swamp dwellers hereabouts are quite agreeable – even helpful, I might say!'

Grobwold paused for effect.

'There *is* a way through – they told me!'

Case, Marcus and the others exchanged glances.

'Grobwold, are you sure?' asked Case. 'Can we really trust them?'

'With your own grandmother, my dear chap!' he beamed. 'No problem!'

The Albard were none too keen, but in the clear absence of a plausible alternative, they decided they should make the attempt. Within a few minutes, they were gathered at the edge of the swamp and looking uncertainly at each other. Only Case and the Brendel seemed unconcerned. As Marcus pulled on his main pack, his shoulder bag fell to the ground, spilling out the sphere. It was glowing bright green!

'Case – look!' he shouted.

Case took one glance and stared about him looking this way and that. Suddenly he stiffened, pointing up the mountainside.

'There!' he yelled.

Looking up, they all saw it – a dark, seething mass filled the upper slopes, seeming to pour out of the very mountainside itself. It was moving rapidly, a black army swarming like ants towards them. A few moments later, they began to hear the clattering of weapons and a baying that filled their hearts with fear. Mesmerised, the Search watched as hundreds and hundreds of Greblocks surged towards them.

'Quick!' yelled Case, again. 'Into the swamp!'

Needing no further bidding and waiting only for Marcus to pick up the sphere and replace it in his bag, they hurried after Grobwold into the swirling mists ahead. Looking back fearfully, they could see Greblocks teeming onto the lower slopes, now only a matter of minutes behind them. All around them, the limpid mud swirled and plopped. Gnarled roots and knotted creepers threatened to trip them at every step as if trying to pitch the fleeing figures into that fearful quagmire. They pushed on as fast as Grobwold's trail would allow, preferring the dangers of the swamp to the unthinkable monstrosities that pursued them. After another few minutes, Grobwold stopped and turned.

'That should be far enough!' he announced. 'I want to see this!'

'What are you doing?' shouted Case. 'For pity's sake, keep going!'

'Don't worry, old thing!' soothed Grobwold. 'Look!'

The front line of advancing Greblocks had reached the edge of the swamp, where they hesitated. More and more arrived, crowding up behind them. Without warning, the Greblocks became silent and still. They appeared to be listening – waiting for some kind of instruction. Suddenly, as if they had been switched back on, they all began yelling and rattling their weapons together. Some of them shot great bolts of flame into the sky from the ends of their spears until, as a single unit, they surged into the swamp. They slipped in up to their waists, some being trampled under by those behind in their eagerness to continue in pursuit of their prey. Soon, the entire swarm of Greblocks was surging through the swamp straight towards them, slowed by the thick mud but pressing on nevertheless.

Case gripped Grobwold's elbow, panic rising in him.

'Grobwold!' he hissed. 'We must get out of here—*now*!'

'What! And miss the best bit?' he cried. 'Not likely!'

At that moment, something in the swamp stirred. Something very large. The bloodthirsty clamouring from the Greblocks changed into shrieks of fear as a gigantic head, seemingly all mouth and teeth, rose in their midst. Then another, and another, until there was a dozen or more.

'Meet the cavalry!' beamed Grobwold, craning his neck to get a better view.

What followed was utter carnage. The beasts from the swamp chomped, bit and chewed their way through the entire stranded army, roaring in thunderous delight as they went about their gruesome business until not a single Greblock was left. One by one, the feeders, making sure they had missed nothing, slipped satisfied back under the surface of the churned and black stained mud.

'Well done, boys and girls!' called Grobwold across the swamp. 'Well done! First class!'

Although quite numb from the spectacle of what they had just witnessed, the company felt no pity. Something more like relief, as they considered the fate that would certainly have overtaken them had those wretched creatures caught up.

'Two birds with one stone!' exclaimed Grobwold, satisfied.

'What do you mean?' asked Marcus.

'Because, my friend, they have fair done for that lot,' he answered, 'and now they're too full to bother us!'

Case shot Grobwold a sideways glance.

'I thought you said it was safe in here!'

'Well, I did say there were one or two unsavoury characters around,

121

didn't I!' he grinned.

Marcus looked in his bag. The was no glow from the sphere, a fact that he reported to Case.

'Good!' he smiled. 'Time to press on wouldn't you say! Come on Grobwold – let's get out of here!'

Keeping a very wary eye on the surrounding swamp, the party followed its pathfinder in single file and silence. They need not have worried. That intimidating place proved to be harmless, just as Grobwold had said it would be. As evening approached, they came to the banks of a huge river, cutting a swathe through the swamp as it flowed towards the sea.

'This is going to be a problem!' observed Case, staring across the wide expanse.

'We'll see about that in the morning!' chipped in Grobwold, cheerfully.

Case decided not to ask the question he wanted to, trusting that Grobwold had something in mind and not forgetting that he had single handedly saved all of their skins that day. Instead, Case simply smiled at him.

'I am *very* pleased you decided to come with us, Grobwold!' he declared.

'All in a day's work!' returned Grobwold, delighted at the compliment. 'I still prefer my kitchen though!' he added, grinning.

They slept well that night, in spite of the nightmarish Greblock slaughter they had witnessed, waking refreshed and ready for whatever difficulties the new day might bring. They did not have to wait long for their first challenge. Grobwold had moved off to the edge of the river and was gabbling unintelligibly across the water. A short while later, two turtle-like creatures bobbed to the surface nearby.

The two enormous amphibians clawed their way on to the riverbank while Grobwold organised everyone except himself on to their broad, leathery backs. Moments later, with Grobwold swimming alongside, they were crossing the river. Someone had to fall in – and it was General, of course! He was acting the fool by standing up on the slippery turtle shell and shading his eyes to the far bank, shouting 'Land ho!' It came as no surprise when he tumbled headfirst into the current. In a moment, he had disappeared below the surface, with Grobwold after him like a flash. Seconds later, although it seemed very much longer, he was pushed, spluttering and gasping, back with the others, amid howls of laughter and feeling very sorry for himself.

'Serves yer right, Captain General!' taunted Richmane, prompting renewed hoots of laughter.

They reached the far bank without further incident and, aside from General and Grobwold, reasonably dry. After Grobwold had garbled his thanks and waved his farewells to the turtles, they set off once more. The Wampurian picked his way through the still dangerous swamp with great care, until, midway through the afternoon they found firmer ground. Within an hour, they were clear of the swamp and climbing a gentle, sandy slope tufted with hardy looking vegetation. Shortly, they crested a small ridge and stood staring at the panorama that presented itself.

'The Shadowlands!' whispered Case. 'I never thought I'd live to see the day . . .

'The scenery was unlike anything any of them had ever seen before. A huge, flat sandy desert, interspersed with rocky outcrops and deep

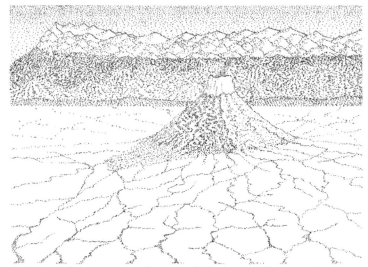

crevices and canyons stretched out before them. They could see the Curtains running from behind them in a huge arc to the north, where they disappeared into the distance. But the dominant feature was a huge, snow-capped volcano rising majestically out of the centre of the surrounding desert, perfectly conical except for the jagged line of its smoking and still active crater.

Chapter 11 - The Desert

Fascinated and fearful, the company stared at the volcano. A shimmering heat haze from the desert before them made it appear to float, somehow separate from the plain, its distant lower slopes almost the same colour as the background. Only the snow covering higher up stood out in detail. Columns of smoke rose ominously from its crater.

The Brendel soon confirmed that this was their objective. In the meantime, they had two major problems to overcome. First, they would need water, and plenty of it, to cross that vast tract of sand and rock. Second, they did not want to be seen – especially by Greblocks!

Deciding to take stock of their situation, they moved back down the ridge, facing the swamps they had just crossed.

'Out o' the soup kettle an' into the fire!' observed General, adequately summing up their situation.

Case estimated that it would take at least five or six days to cross that terrain, even if they found no natural obstacles. He did not like the look of the deep fissures that spread across the desert and was worried they would hinder progress.

'So,' he concluded, 'between the desert and the Greblocks, we seem to have come to another stop. We can't carry enough water with us and the prospects of finding any out there don't seem too good. It seems to me that the only thing we can do is to skirt around the edge of the desert and try again from the north.'

'But Case, that could take weeks, an' we don't 'ave near enough supplies to last that long,' objected Udiger.

The other Albard nodded their agreement.

Case thought for a while.

'Perhaps we can find enough to keep us going along the way,' he suggested. 'You know, fruits and berries – that sort of thing.'

He did not sound too convincing.

'It's likely we'll 'ave to cross the same sort o' ground from the north – even if we do manage to get that far,' put in General to the accompaniment of more assenting nods.

'But we can't just give up now!' urged Case. 'We have to go on – somehow. At least let's make a start and take a look at what's out there. We've still got a couple of hours before nightfall.'

Wearily and without much hope, the Quest rose to their feet and pulled on their packs. Marcus reported that all was quiet as far as the sphere was concerned and they trudged off keeping out of sight of the desert just below the sandy ridge, with the marsh to their left and heading west into the reddening sun.

As they proceeded, the marsh gradually dried up and the scrub that replaced it gradually gave way to scattered woodland, mostly pine. Between them and the coast, which they knew to be some way to the east, forested hills began to rise steadily upwards to yet more mountains. Once in a while, one or other of the Albard would move to the top of the ridge to keep an eye on the desert, but each time, they reported no change. When it started to get dark, the party moved down towards the trees and set up camp for the night. Before they ate, it was decided to spread out their rations, so they could estimate roughly how long they could expect them to last. After considerable deliberation, they agreed that they had enough for about four weeks.

This was a sobering thought, for as they checked Case's maps, they realised it would take at least that long to get back to Marchant. There would be no 'Liberty' waiting for them in Wrackwater Sound and they would have to cover the entire distance on foot.

'Point o' no return, then!' remarked General, who had developed a knack for stating the obvious.

Feeling stranded and vulnerable, they ate what little they had allowed themselves for supper. Still hungry, they settled themselves down for the night, to sleep on the decision they knew would have to be made in the morning.

First light saw Case, Linden and Hornbeam in earnest, silent conversation once more. Something was amiss, that was clear, but everyone had to wait patiently until they were finished.

It was a grim-faced Case that reported a few minutes later to the still sleepy risers.

'Something's out there,' he informed them, indicating the desert with a nod of his head. 'And its coming this way! The Brendel don't know what it is, but they have picked up signs.'

On hearing this, Marcus checked the sphere.

'Not Greblocks, anyway!' he offered.

'Well that's something, at least!' smiled Grobwold, trying to stay cheerful and to comfort Jade at the same time. She was looking tired and frightened.

'What can we do, Case?' asked Marcus, beginning to feel afraid himself.

He had already been looking around, trying to decide just that.

'The trees!' he pointed. 'We'll hide in the trees. Come on!'

The group hurried further into the woodland until they found three or four climbable trees growing close together. A few moments later, they were concealed high up in their branches, surrounded by sharp needles and pine cones oozing with a strong scented, sticky sap – all except for Grobwold, who had decided that the shelter of a nearby boulder would do for him. He just wasn't built for climbing trees!

From their hiding place, they could see the ridge and the top of the huge volcano towering into the sky, but not the desert itself. They did not have long to wait. Something moved away to their right.

'There!' whispered Case, pointing.

Eleven pairs of eyes watched from the cover of their branches as, one by one, several heads appeared over the ridge. Soon there were a dozen or more, looking around them. Were it not for the fact that the ridge was on the skyline, they doubted they'd have seen them at all, strange, shaggy looking heads, blending almost perfectly with the sand. Soon, like so many ghosts, they tumbled silently down the sandy slope, gaining their feet as they came to the path the travellers had trodden the night before. They gathered together, inspecting and prodding the ground with their spears, constantly looking about themselves and sniffing the air. Moments later, they began to spread along the track, some erect and some on all fours, moving ever closer towards the trees that concealed the Search. With rising alarm, the party saw them becoming excited and agitated as they found the place they had decided earlier to spend the night, pointing here and there at the tell-tale signs. Marcus could see them clearly now – ape-like, tailless creatures, with maned wolfish looking heads. Against the woodland carpet, they stood out distinctly. He could see by their colouring that they would be practically invisible in their natural desert habitat.

One of their number separated from the rest, staring hard at the ground. Moments later, a pair of yellow, intelligent eyes looked upwards, peering directly into the thick foliage above. Case looked apprehensively towards Linden and Hornbeam, who signalled back that, as yet, they had not been able to establish the intentions of these creatures,

Meanwhile, the wolf-thing called to the others in a gruff, throaty growl and jabbing its spear upwards. Slowly, weapons at the ready and looking straight up at them, the desert dwellers circled the clump of trees.

The two groups stared at one another for a long time, neither moving, each trying to weigh up the other. It was Grobwold who broke the stalemate. Lumbering from behind his boulder like some great prehistoric beast, he charged down on the startled creatures. Recovering quickly from their initial surprise, they scattered in all directions, ducking behind whatever cover they could find. But they stood their ground, watching Grobwold warily as he circled the clump of trees protectively, bellowing fearfully – until the Brendel signalled him to stay still.

Linden and Hornbeam swung down easily from the branches, dropped lightly to the floor and sat down beside Grobwold. Not knowing what to make of this intervention, he stopped roaring and sat down himself.

They sat patiently, until one of the wolf-things moved cautiously from its cover, keeping its eyes firmly fixed on Grobwold as it advanced. Finally, it sat down opposite the Brendel, laying its spear to one side.

Linden and Hornbeam concentrated hard, trying to find a way into the complex mind that sat before them. For its part, the wolf-thing kept moving its head from side to side, its ears flicking this way and that, as if trying to catch some elusive sound drifting on the breeze. Finally, as if a key had turned in a stubborn lock, they opened a way through. The creature looked surprised and shook its head roughly, as if trying to rid itself of an unwelcome irritation. Then it seemed to realise that the intrusion into its mind was coming directly from the strange looking pair seated before him.

'We are Brendel and we mean you no harm.'

The wolf-thing looked at Grobwold and then back to Linden and Hornbeam.

'Him neither!' they reassured.

'We are Sandroamers and we mean you no harm, either. Just curious as to who it is approaching our homes,' he returned as both thought and speech, for the benefit of the others who had come out of their cover and gathered behind him.

'I am Linden,' he projected, 'and this is Hornbeam.'

The Sandroamer pointed at himself and said 'Ghark.'

Slowly and deliberately, he pointed towards the Brendel, Grobwold and up into the trees. Finally, he spread his hands with a shrug. He was clearly trying to make a connection between the strange mixture of beings that made up the group.

'We are travelling together,' responded Linden.

'Where to?'

'To the Smoking Mountain!'

'Why?'

'We are in search of something!'

'What, exactly?'

'That, friend, is a very long story!'

Up in the branches, Case had been following everything.

'Come on!' he called to the others and leading the way. 'Time to go down!'

One by one, each member of the Search dropped down from the branches and stood with Grobwold and the Brendel, facing the band of Sandroamers. Case stepped forward.

'I am Case,' he began. 'This is Marcus, Jade and the Albard. Together, we have journeyed from the other side of the great mountains, a long and difficult way from here. I apologise for coming uninvited, but we seek something of great importance to us all.'

'Treasure hunters!' growled Ghark, showing his wicked looking teeth.

'No, Ghark. We are searching for a person. The one we call Marchman and we believe he is held prisoner somewhere on your volcano, over there,' he said, looking upwards.

'We seek him because we have something of his that must be returned. Without it, Marchman cannot protect our world from the forces of evil that have arrived here. Unless we succeed, I fear all our days are numbered.'

'Forces of evil?' grunted Ghark.

'Greblocks – and whatever controls them!' answered Case.

'The Black-eyed Ones!' he growled. 'We have seen them.'

Ghark nodded, along with the other Sandroamers behind him.

'In the desert?' asked Case.

Ghark nodded again. 'They are bad!' he added.

There was silence for a while. Finally, Ghark stood up, clearly having come to a decision,

'We take you to Smoking Mountain,' he said, indicating the distant volcano. 'Stay night here. Follow us in morning!'

Despite the many unanswered questions still to be asked on both sides, it was a promising alliance and the group that spread itself around the clearing close to the edge of the desert that night slept the better for it.

*   *   *

Now that the Search had joined forces with their new Sandroamer allies, they entered the desert at first light, led by Ghark and heading towards their objective. After a short but difficult route through sand dunes, they came to one of the deep cracks that they had seen criss-crossing the desert the day before. The Sandroamers disappeared into it, beckoning the Search to follow. It was a tricky and sometimes perilous descent, but soon everyone was safely down at the bottom, out of the bright sunshine and into cool shade. On they pressed, the sides of the ravine towering above them. From time to time, they had to clamber over rock falls and slither up and down steeper sections. Occasionally, their way offered a choice of paths, but the Sandroamers always seemed to know which to take.

The Search became tired and dusty as the day wore on. Worse, their meagre supplies of drinking water were beginning to run out.

Case went ahead and stopped Ghark as they approached another fork in the path.

'Please!' he said. 'We must rest. We also need water!'

Ghark clapped his hands. Immediately, the Sandroamers scattered,

shortly to return with small, pear-shaped pods in their arms that they had unearthed here and there. They were passed around. Ghark showed them what to do, biting off the narrow end, tipping the contents into his mouth and swallowing. The others followed suit, and feeling much refreshed, they resumed their trek, pockets filled with the precious pods. As night began to fall, the Sandroamers turned up a small crevice that soon widened into a deep canyon. Ghark pointed out a series of dark openings just ahead.

'Shelter!' he grunted.

Soon, they were in a series of interlinking caves or burrows – they could not decide which. There was something unnatural about them, as if they had been made, for whatever reason. Down there, deep below the surface of the desert and away from the prying eyes of the Greblocks and whatever else was up there, they felt secure. Grobwold had gathered, with the help of the Sandroamers, great armfuls of dried scrub. Soon, a good fire was going. Although the expedition offered to share their food, the Sandroamers were quite content with their pods, seeming to need little else. Outside the caves, the night desert air became cold, but the tired travellers were kept warm by the fire and their blankets and slept well.

Next morning, they were awakened by the Sandroamers, who appeared to have been up and around for quite a time. Bleary eyed and footsore from the previous day's exertions over the difficult and rocky terrain, they grabbed what they could by way of breakfast and gathered their things together. Shortly afterwards, they continued their scrambling journey and struggling to keep pace with their guides.

There was only one noteworthy incident that day, but nonetheless frightening for that! As the party filed through a narrow gorge, Marcus had noticed a series of small, round tunnels in the rock, like rabbit burrows, except that it would take some rabbit to scrape one of those out! Suddenly, from somewhere up ahead, there was a shout. It was General – and he was clearly in serious trouble. Something foul and unspeakable had struck at him from one of the holes, something that already had his arm in its mouth. Its gelatinous body writhed and rippled as it tried to drag him into its lair. It seemed to be swallowing him, bit by bit, as its mouth and throat worked their way up his arm. Despite his struggles, general was slowly disappearing before their horrified eyes, as the giant worm-like monster slithered its top jaw over his head, seemingly in attempt to swallow him whole before crushing him and sliding back into its hole.

The Sandroamers were quick to respond. Pushing their way back along the narrow crevice to the unfortunate General, they speared the monster sideways through its body and out on the other side, which prevented it from retreating into its hole. Then, with a Sandroamer at each end of the spear, they heaved outwards, bracing their feet on the rock. A third Sandroamer thrust his spear through the newly exposed, squirming flanks, and once more they heaved, revealing more of the monster's body. Another spear and another heave pulled it clear. Ghark stood, spear poised above the writhing and thrashing worm. He found what he was looking for and down went the spear, piercing a dark spot inside the beast. Immediately, it went limp and the Sandroamers set about cutting General free with their knives. He was still alive, but very much the worse for wear, having suffered not just near suffocation, but quite bad lacerations to his arm, neck and head. Quickly, they shouldered him away from that gallery of death, to a safer place just a little further on.

Emdren busied himself cleaning up General's wounds while Jade bathed his face and forehead. Meanwhile, some of the Sandroamers hurried off in search of something Ghark had sent them for. The remainder set about cutting up the rock worm. Soon, the Sandroamer searchers returned, one of them carrying a handful of strong smelling leaves which Ghark proceeded to pound between two rocks. Adding some of the juice from one of the yellow pods, he mixed up a paste which, as soon as it was ready, he began to spread over General's open wounds.

'Take out poison!' he grunted at Emdren, who began to bandage him up as soon as the Sandroamer had finished.

A little while later, surrounded by anxious faces, General regained consciousness and opened his eyes. He closed them again, with a shudder of relief.

'Thought I was a goner there!' he whispered, feebly.

'You're safe now, General. Take it easy,' comforted Case, patting him on his good shoulder.

While they waited for General to recover, the Sandroamers sat around devouring pieces of the rock worm. Its flesh looked decidedly unsavoury, but they appeared to relish it. Before long, there was nothing left, save for the skin and a few sinews.

General's recovery was as rapid as it was unexpected. The ointment prepared by Ghark had done its work and he was standing, insisting that he was well enough to continue. Moving off once more, they continued their trek, keeping a wary eye out for holes in the rock as they went.

That evening, they found more tunnels to shelter in. Case wandered up and down, examining the walls with great curiosity.

'These tunnels aren't natural, are they?' he asked Ghark.

He shook his head.

'Who made them?' persisted Case.

'We did!' answered Ghark.

'Why?'

'Looking for these,' he stated, producing something his hand as if from nowhere. It was a piece of blue crystal.

'What is it?' asked Case again.

'Does things. Show you tomorrow.'

With that, Ghark put away the stone. Case realised that the conversation was at an end, at least for the moment. He re-joined the others and listened for a while to General retelling his encounter with the rock worm. The Albard were getting a little tired of hearing about it over and over, and their earlier sympathy for General had just about run out.

'Can't yer jus' shurrup, worm-bait?' interrupted Welgar playfully. Good natured laughter brightened up the fire-lit faces, the more so when one of the Sandroamers asked if they could use him to catch another rock worm tomorrow. None of this bothered General. He liked being the centre of attention even if it did mean a bit of teasing.

Next morning, Case got the demonstration of the usefulness of the skystone that Ghark had promised. They had been pushing along for about two hours, when Ghark called a halt and gestured Case to a patch of sunlight that angled into the depths of the ravine through a cleft on the surface. Gathering some dry vegetation together, he set the skystone carefully in the middle of it, to catch the sun's rays. Seconds later, a tiny curl of smoke rose, followed by a flicker of flame which Ghark had soon coaxed into life, deftly removing the stone as he did so.

'Impressive!' remarked Case.

'Not all,' replied Ghark. Taking a slingshot from his pouch, he fitted the skystone into it. Taking careful aim, he whirled it around his head and let fly at a distant cactus. The stone hummed as it sped across the canyon. A second or two later, the projectile struck its mark, gouging a large hole in the stem of the plant. It teetered for a moment, before toppling to the ground.

'Hunting!' grinned Ghark.

At the Sandroamer's beckoning, Case followed him to the top of the

ravine, crossing the canyon and collecting the skystone as they went. As they neared the top, Ghark gestured for Case to stay low. As the two of them cautiously put their heads above the edge, they could see the sun-baked surface of the desert stretching away from them. Case noted with satisfaction that they were much closer to the volcano and his nose twitched as it caught faint traces of sulphur in the air.

'Watch!' Ghark held the skystone in the sunlight, twisting it from side to side. Moments later, and from a great distance somewhere of the left flank of the volcano, he saw a rapid series of flashes being returned.

'Suntalk!' grunted Ghark. 'All clear!'

Case had seen enough. This was indeed a useful stone. They scrambled back down to the others, who had been watching with proceedings with interest, as well as being glad of the break.

That day, and the next, passed without incident. Ghark disappeared off to the rim of the canyon more and more frequently in order to check with distant Sandroamers that their way was still clear, using their 'suntalk'.

Later, as they gained the safety of another series of old skystone workings to spend the night, Ghark called them together. As they sat comfortably around the fire, he spoke.

'Two more days, at Smoking Mountain,' he announced, looking around. 'But not safe!'

He continued, eyes flashing in the firelight.

'Black-eyed Ones – patrols – guarding mountain.'

Case and the rest of the Search looked at one another.

'Is there another way through?' he asked.

Ghark nodded. 'But dangerous. Not easy!'

With his finger, he traced a crooked line in the sand on the tunnel floor, at the end of which he outlined the volcano, complete with smoke. Then he prodded some indentations in a quick-fire series of jabs.

'Ravine, us,' he growled, pointing at the crooked line.

'Smoking Mountain,' he added, indicating his outline.

Then he pointed at the indentations he'd made. 'Tunnels. Go deep— many skystones!'

'And the Greblocks?' asked Case.

'All over. But not in tunnels,' came the answer.

'So, we can get *into* the volcano, but not on it,' murmured Case. 'Well, that's something, anyway.'

'Marchman?' Ghark grunted, looking at him.

Case's eyes lighted on Linden and Hornbeam for a while.

'He's there! Somewhere . . .'

They sat quietly, minds full of what they might expect over the next few days. Would they be able to find Marchman? And what else lay waiting for them?

Sleep did not come easily that night.

Chapter 12 - Smoking Mountain

Setting off at first light, they took great care not to make any unnecessary noise. Casual conversation was frowned upon as they picked their way along the desert fissures and it soon stopped altogether, concentrating instead on keeping their footing. Stops were kept to the bare minimum and they made good progress. Case accompanied Ghark on several occasions up to the rim of the desert to confirm that all was still well. The Sandroamers were proving expert in their own terrain and Case was convinced that their presence had, so far, gone undetected by the Greblocks.

On their last trip to the top, Ghark had assured Case that they would reach the foot of Smoking Mountain by the end of the next day. Everyone was now feeling the tension and they spent another restless night, tossing and turning in their blankets. The following morning, they set out on what they hoped would be the last leg of their journey. According to Case's diary, this was the twenty sixth day since leaving Stonefort. As they moved silently along, Marcus reflected on that. He could hardly believe that, in the early days, he had thought all this to be a dream! His mind raced through each stage of their travels, from the plains south of Middlemere and the gale, into the forests of the Brendel and out through Flower Vale down to Marchant, where they had boarded the 'Liberty'. He recalled the discomfort caused by the storm, their crossing of the Bay of Whales and through to Wrackwater Sound, where they put ashore. He shuddered as he remembered the slaughter in the swamp and smiled at the memory of General falling in the river! Then it was hiding from the Sandroamers and the seemingly endless journey through desert ravines and canyons – not forgetting General's almost fatal encounter with the rock worm! And here they were, almost at journey's end.

His head was full of what he imagined might lie ahead when there was sudden alarm at the front of the line. The word to lie still was passed back and everyone settled against the floor of the canyon, confident that their grimed and dusty bodies were perfectly invisible against the sand. Having no way of knowing what the danger was made it worse, but each of them supposed there were Greblocks nearby. Marcus scolded himself for not checking the sphere as often as he should and took a quick look at it. Sure enough, it was gently pulsating with that all too familiar glow. It seemed like an age before Ghark, almost like a figment of the imagination, glided effortlessly up to the edge of the canyon to look around. Satisfied with what he saw, he re-joined them and announced that all was now clear. It had indeed been a passing Greblock patrol. The group moved on, doubly alert, with Marcus peeping at the sphere every few minutes. He wasn't going to be caught out again.

By nightfall, they had reached Smoking Mountain and taken refuge deep inside one of the acrid smelling tunnels that ran into it. The walls were dotted here and there with skystones, left where they were having been

142

deemed too small to be useful. They shed a faint, blue light, just sufficient to light their way.

The Brendel were becoming agitated. Case sat with them for a while before returning to the others, looking concerned.

'Marchman is here,' he whispered. 'Somewhere above us, but his thoughts are weakening rapidly. Wherever he is, he's in great distress and . . .' Case paused, looking around, ' . . . and close to death! We don't have much time!'

After another hurried consultation, they decided to press on. Linden and Hornbeam led the way with Ghark and Case close behind. Whenever the tunnels divided, or a passageway ran off to one side or the other, Ghark was on hand to say which were clear and which were dead ends. Whenever there was a choice, Linden and Hornbeam made the decision. In this way, the Search moved deeper and deeper into the volcano, climbing steadily as they went. From time to time, the Brendel stopped, concentrated hard and pressed forward with renewed energy. The urgency shown by Linden and Hornbeam spread quickly through to everyone else, their senses heightening with every step.

It was beginning to get warm. Sweat stood out on foreheads as they moved on, breathing hard as they penetrated further and further into the heart of Smoking Mountain.

Marcus looked in his bag and saw the sphere glowing brightly. He caught up with Case to show him. Instantly he called a halt. As they waited in silence, everyone listened intently but there was not a sound to be heard. Ghark suggested that they should now proceed with greater care, sending two Sandroamers ahead each time to make sure the way was clear, with one of them returning to tell them it was safe to carry on. For what seemed hours, they continued like this. Meanwhile, the sphere glowed more and more brightly, even shining through its leather bag. Their nerves were almost in shreds when Ghark came hurrying back from one of his forward forays.

'Lights up ahead!' he growled. 'Black-eyed Ones. Coming this way!'

Desperately, they looked around. A little way back, they had passed a tunnel. A dead end, Ghark had told them. Losing no time, they started back towards it, turning in thankfully and moving some way inside to take advantage of the darkness it offered. They sat and settled down to wait. Almost sick with anxiety, they heard the approaching crunch, crunch of Greblocks on the march. To their intense relief, they heard them pass until all sounds of their footsteps had faded completely. Waiting for another few minutes, they crept out from their hiding place and continued along the tunnel the Greblocks had just marched down.

When they reached approximately the same place as before, Ghark moved on ahead. When he returned, he looked puzzled.

'Light still there!' he said. 'But not from one of our tunnels.'

'What do you mean?' asked Case.

'We not make this one,' he answered.

This time, it was Case who went ahead to see for himself. Sure enough, there was the glow, lighting up the tunnel from some way off. He noted that the tunnel walls were different, somehow. Smoother. He went back to the others and they moved off until they could all see it for themselves. Slowly and carefully, they crept nearer until they could make out the end of the tunnel they were in. Whatever lay beyond was the source of the light. Step by step, they advanced until finally, they were within a few paces of its edge.

By now, the sphere was glowing so brightly that Marcus had to wrap it in his blanket to prevent it from filling the entire place with its green light. Even then, some of it filtered through, pulsating harder than ever. Finally, he lay himself across it as he crawled to the end of the tunnel.

Running down from them was a curving ramp leading into an enormous cavern. The walls sparkled with skystones, clustered thickly together and shedding the most brilliant light everywhere. It was incredibly beautiful and drew gasps of admiration, even from the Sandroamers who

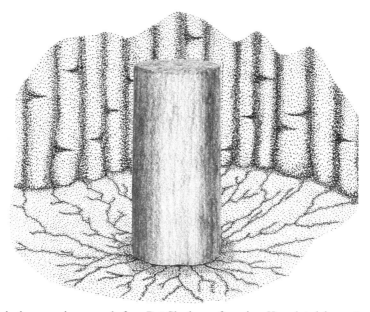

had seen such caverns before. But Ghark was frowning. He pointed down at a smooth, cylindrical piece of black rock.

'Not belong here!' he growled at Case.

Realising that the Greblock patrol they had just narrowly avoided must have come this way, they were aware that the utmost caution was needed at this moment. Slowly and carefully, they descended the ramp until they were on the floor of that magnificent place. Straight away, Ghark made his way to the black cylinder, which stood quite as high as himself and seemed to grow from the very floor itself. The others gathered around, just as curious.

Quite without warning, the walls around them became alive. As they slid quietly and menacingly from their places of concealment, the cavern became lined with Greblocks, black eyes glinting with venom and hatred.

It did not take a tactical genius to work out they were trapped – hopelessly and utterly.

Chapter 13 - The Emperor of Darkness

Strangely enough, a kind of relief swept over them. Having lived the moment of capture so many times in their minds, now it had happened, they were not afraid. More like a feeling of resignation, yet at the same time, angry for walking into such an obvious trap. The Sandroamers stood around, facing the leering Greblocks, defensive and alert, but making no attempt to move towards them. It was unnerving to watch them just standing there. Case looked up just in time to see the same Greblock patrol that had passed them earlier arrive back at the tunnel entrance at the top of the ramp, blocking their last chance of escape. Not that he thought there would have been much hope of reaching it anyway.

'End of the line, I fear!' he said, looking sadly down at Marcus. Looking around again, he added, 'We seem to be expecting someone!'

They did not have long to wait, for a few seconds later, a faint glow appeared on the top surface of the black cylinder in front of them. Rapidly, the emanation began to grow outwards and upwards, until a sinister column of green light extended vertically to the roof of the cavern. The shaft of light filled with flecks of green, black and blue flecks that swirled erratically. Out of the corner of his eye, Case saw the Greblocks move slightly, as they stiffened in anticipation of what was coming. He, however, was quite unprepared for what happened next. Something began to materialise inside the column, something tall and dark, absorbing the dancing specks as it grew. Finally, it stood there, fully formed, arms folded and bathed in a sickening pale green hue.

They stared, uncomprehending and yet fascinated at what seemed to be the manifestation of evil itself. It looked human, except for its size, which was easily twice the height of a normal man. Yet clearly it was not human, for its face had a puffy, reptilian look with slick black hair that swept from its forehead between three crested ridges and an absence of ears. Its nose bore a pair of wide nostrils beneath which was a long, curving sweep of flesh leading down to its mouth. A mouth that seemed cruelty itself, thin and pitiless, and set in a thick square jaw that heightened the effect. It was clothed in something that resembled soft leather, except that it moved in a tiny series of ripples, spreading and interlocking continuously as if it had a life of its own.

Marcus stole a look at the Sphere of Light that he could feel pulsating wildly. Its light streamed out from the folds of the blanket, casting vivid green patches on the floor of the cavern around his feet. Nervously, he pulled the blanket tighter, doing his best to keep it covered.

Without warning, the apparition's eyes snapped open, fiery red and contemptuous, sliding around the cavern and taking in every detail. Fixing the hapless intruders with a sudden rotation of its head and a long, malevolent stare, it spoke.

148

'Welcome, weary travellers. And bringing with you the thing that has eluded the best efforts of my army! How very kind of you!'

It was a grating, hissing voice, laced with spite and mockery and sending a shiver down every spine. Jade whimpered and buried her face in Grobwold's side.

'This belongs to me, I believe!' it grated, pointing at the bundle held closely by Marcus.

'It's not yours!' challenged Marcus indignantly, fighting back the fear that gnawed his very insides out.

'The boy has spirit!' it laughed. A cruel, hollow laugh, completely devoid of humour.

'Then to whom *does* it belong?' it continued in a tone of mock patience, while bringing a hand up to its face to examine its shining claws as if to express only a casual interest in the answer.

'Be careful, Marcus!' warned Case.

The claw dropped back to its side.

'Be careful?' it thundered. 'Be careful!' The cavern reverberated with the resounding echo, battering their ears.

'And who is *this* that dares to interrupt the Emperor of Darkness?' Its tone had changed completely to a sinister and threatening whisper, its eyes settling on Case.

Case stood his ground, defiance in his eyes.

The Emperor of Darkness smiled evilly. Extending an arm and pointing a claw, a stream of dense black particles flew across the cavern engulfing Case. His face became a mask of agony.

'You amuse me!' he grated, with glittering eyes lingering on his victim and looking anything but amused.

149

'A further demonstration of my powers!' it hissed.

Looking away from Case, his gaze settled on one of the Greblocks. In an instant, it was engulfed in flames and, moments later, all that remained was a scorch on the cavern wall above a smouldering, bubbling black pool where the unfortunate creature had been standing. The other Greblocks were unmoved, while horrified looks were exchanged between members of the Search.

'So—you now see that I have total control over *everything* and *everyone*. Resisting my will is pure folly!' leered the Emperor. 'Now, where was I? Ah, yes – the boy!'

His triumphant gaze settled once more upon Marcus. From somewhere behind him, Jade slipped a hand into his, which he found comforting.

'You were about to explain something to me, I recall. Something about a dispute of ownership. Please go on – I am fascinated!'

The Emperor of Darkness savoured the sound of every single syllable sliding from his cruel lips.

'Let Case go first!' replied Marcus, swallowing back his fear and drawing heavily on the renewed strength that surged through him from Jade's hand.

A flash of anger passed across the red eyes, but subsided almost as quickly.

'As a gesture of goodwill and to demonstrate the compassion and generosity of your host, I shall grant your request!'

These words were lined heavily with sarcasm, the Emperor clearly enjoying his total control and mastery of the situation. With a click of its claws, Case was released, falling to the floor and clutching at his throat, clearly still in great pain. Marcus realised that the Emperor of Darkness could take what he wanted at any time, but he had seen bullies at work before and knew their motives well. They liked to gloat and prolong the agony, just as the Emperor was doing now. It was only when they got tired of the entertainment that they finished things off, like a cat playing with a mouse. Marcus wondered how long he could string things out. For the moment, he decided he would try being straightforward.

'It belongs to Marchman!' he said, firmly.

'What does?' mocked the Emperor. 'What *precisely* are we talking about?

The tips of his claws came together in front of his chin, feigning nonchalance.

Marcus immediately switched tactics to see if he could further divert his adversary.

'It's a piece of treasure known as the Heart of Galidian,' he answered, surprising himself. His face was a picture of innocence and honesty.

'How *very* interesting!' re-joined the Emperor. 'And please tell me – just what is this 'Heart of Galidian'?' He was clearly enjoying this game immensely, knowing that he was holding all the best cards.

'It's a kind of jewel,' replied Marcus.

'And you say it belongs to Marchman?'

Marcus changed tactics again, this time deciding to play on the Emperor's vanity.

'Yes!' he stated in a matter of fact sort of way.

Before the Emperor had time to come back with another question, Marcus continued.

'I've never seen Marchman. I've heard so much about him but we've never actually met,' he carried on, 'but I don't suppose even *you* could arrange that!'

He smiled sweetly, head on one side, submissive. He'd done all this before with Johnny Prescott and Fred Baines. He'd even got away with it a couple of times.

The Emperor of Darkness knew exactly what was going on but was feeling quite diverted and entertained by it all. Besides, he thought, it would be singularly amusing to watch Marchman's face, contorted and twisted with anguish at finally seeing his precious Sphere of Light fall into his possession.

He smiled an evil and contemptuous smile.

'But nothing could be simpler, child!' he simpered.

His eyes glittered imperiously as he clicked his claws once more, this time in the direction of an opening towards the back of the cavern.

Moments later, two Greblocks appeared, dragging something unceremoniously across the floor. At a command from the Emperor, they released it and retreated.

'Marchman!' he announced with a sweep of his arm.

'Is he quite what you expected, boy?'

The Emperor threw back his head laughing cruelly.

Marcus looked across the expanse of the cavern. The bundle of rags lay there, unmoving.

'Is – Is he dead?' whispered Marcus, his head swimming in despair.

'Not yet, child – not yet!' hissed the Emperor.

Turning once again, he hurled a bolt of shimmering energy at the bundle on the floor. The rags twitched and convulsed with a sharp spasm of

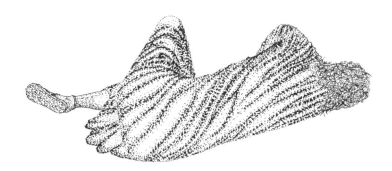

pain. Moments later, a pale bearded face wearing a dismal and tortured expression lifted itself from the floor and stared around, blinking. The pale blue eyes were vacant and unseeing.

'Come now, Marchman. This is no way to receive your visitors. On your feet, I say!' the Emperor goaded. Another bolt flew across the cavern. With a groan of agony that would have melted any heart of stone, Marchman rose, tottering, to his feet, sagging and dangling like a broken puppet.

The Emperor of Darkness stood, arms folded and imperious. His lips were smeared with a triumphant leer. Slowly, his gaze rested back on Marcus, who felt prickles on the back of his neck as the Emperor stretched out a claw towards him.

'Now, child, bring to me what is mine!'

He was irresistible. Fight as he might, Marcus found himself unwrapping the sphere until it lay in his hands, shedding a dazzling green light that filled the cavern with its radiance. Slowly, he found himself edging towards the Emperor's outstretched claw, lifting the sphere as he went.

The Emperor, body and wicked soul thirsting for that which he had sought for so, so long, became entranced by the brilliance of the sphere. And here it was, almost in his grasp. At last!

Suddenly and without anyone realising what was happening, something flew past Marcus and threw itself into the pillar of green light, yelling and swinging its arms as it caught the Emperor around his knees, dislodging him from his pedestal. For an instant, Marcus was released from the spell that had gripped him and the sphere tumbled from his grasp to the floor.

Momentarily, the Emperor of Darkness had looked down to see Jade crashing into him. In his rage and as he recovered his feet, he discharged a bright orange bolt at his assailant, gloating horribly as Jade collapsed into a shapeless bundle at the foot of the cylinder, her life extinguished in a split second.

Before the scowling Emperor could completely recover the situation, Marcus had curled his foot under the sphere and set it rolling and bumping across the cavern floor towards Marchman.

Screaming with fury, the enraged Emperor tried to stop the sphere. In his panic, the bolts from his claws flew wide of their mark, perhaps realising he might destroy the very thing he so cherished. In desperation, he switched his attention to Marchman and let fly with another orange thunderbolt. Marchman ducked down, not to avoid the destructive ball of fire that flew towards him, but to collect the sphere that rolled unerringly into his hands.

As his fingers closed around it, the sphere celebrated with a diamond white flash of such brilliance that all in that place were blinded for

a moment.

When eyes could see again, they saw a new Marchman – tall, strong and in every way fully restored. He and the Emperor of Darkness were circling one another and this time, it was clear to one and all which of them had the upper hand, for the Emperor was retreating, seeking cover wherever he could. The flashes and bolts he let fly were absorbed without so much as a flinch from Marchman as he gradually faced his opponent down. Finally, with nothing else he could do, the Emperor dropped to his knees, whimpering.

Marchman lifted the sphere lovingly in his hands, now shedding a beautiful blue light all around and setting off the skystones in a myriad of twinkling. Holding it before the cowering Emperor, he spoke in a gentle, rich voice that carried to all parts of the cavern.

'Be gone, pestilence!'

Instantly, the Emperor of Darkness began to shrink, as did the Greblocks. They became tiny, bright green sparks that, for a few seconds flew dizzily around the cavern, darting here and there until, one by one, like a showering cascade from some giant firework, they popped faintly until just one remained, bigger and decidedly more active than the rest.

Playfully, Marchman pointed a finger at it and prodded. With a noise like a sharp intake of breath, it too fizzled into nothing.

'Well, strike me down wiv a fevver!' muttered General, not daring to believe his eyes.

Slowly, Marchman turned to the stupefied onlookers, smiling broadly. His eyes twinkled with happiness as he looked them over.

'And who am I to thank for the return of this?' he asked brightly.

Several pairs of eyes picked out Marcus.

Marcus finally found his voice.

'It wasn't just me, sir,' he stammered. 'It was all of us.'

He looked down at the crumpled heap that had been Jade.

'Especially her!' he said, with tears filling his eyes.

Marchman smiled.

'Watch, Marcus!'

He moved the sphere purposefully over the still and lifeless body. Tiny sparks detached themselves from its surface and buried themselves into its scorched flesh. Moments later, a confused but otherwise perfectly healthy Jade pulled herself to her feet.

Marcus looked at Marchman for an instant, hardly daring to believe what he had just witnessed. Next moment, he threw his arms around Jade who was now looking even more confused, not to mention the blushes now reddening her cheeks.

Relieved smiles spread across the faces of the companions as it finally dawned on them that the crisis was over. Galidian was safe! They shook one another's hands and clapped themselves on their backs. Grobwold and General were dancing some kind of jig in their delight, until Grobwold got carried away, lifted him high in the air and planted a big slobbery kiss on his forehead.

Once again, the protesting General was the centre of everyone's amusement.

Chapter 14 - Marchman

The tired but elated friends finally emerged from the tunnels, and spread themselves wearily on the lower slopes of Smoking Mountain in the bright morning sunshine, grateful for the fresh air and a chance to grab a bite to eat. They were far too excited to think of catching up with lost sleep and were having an interesting time listening to Marchman.

He was explaining many things to them. More than a month earlier, he had detected the presence of the Forces of Darkness on Galidian and came down to investigate.

'And sure enough,' he said. 'The Emperor of Darkness had made himself quite at home, here. But I made the mistake of underestimating him and became careless, almost costing – well almost costing everything!'

He smiled, somewhat ruefully, rubbing his bearded chin.

'You see, I believed that the sphere was powerless in his hands, not realising that somehow, somewhere he had learned some of its secrets. Harmless enough, if I had but known! Anyway, he challenged me to a sort of duel. Winner takes all! What I did not realise was that he had a sphere of his own. Not like this one, of course, but potent enough in its own way. I was taken by surprise and lost control, just for an instant. In the struggle that followed, I managed to destroy his sphere, but dropped my own. Away it went, rolling and bouncing down the mountainside – somewhere up there.'

Marchman paused to look up at the Curtains, high to his left.

'The rest is simple. I was overpowered and dragged here by the Greblocks. It was a difficult time. During that journey, I sent out thoughts to every corner of Galidian, hoping beyond hope that somehow, somewhere, *someone* would hear. It is fortunate for us all that these thoughts were gathered – by Case, the Albard and the Brendel. Otherwise, I fear . . .'

He paused again, not wishing to elaborate on what might have happened had the Emperor prevailed.

'Now, if you will please excuse me for a moment, I have something important to do.'

Taking out the sphere, Marchman peered into it. Just as Marcus remembered, it began to glow and shed its dull exterior. Moments later, Ben's rather cross face appeared, eyes roaming all over the place, squinting.

'So, it's you Marchman,' he wheezed. 'About time – I see you've found it, then!'

'Thanks to Marcus and his friends, yes. Just reporting in to say that all's well that ends well, Ben.'

'Yes, well don't be so careless next time,' he scolded, wagging a finger at Marchman.

'And young man!' He shifted position, looking directly at Marcus with his face cracking into a broad smile.

'Well done my boy – well done indeed!'

With that, Ben signed off and the sphere returned to its dormant state. Marchman put it away.

'That's the first time I've seen Ben smile!' he remarked.

'Perhaps you would like to know how you managed to raise Ben before?' Marchman smiled at Marcus.

Marcus nodded. 'I was wondering.' he smiled back shyly.

'The last thing I did before losing contact with the sphere, was to throw a thought, which locked it. Even if the Emperor had found it, the power of the sphere would have eluded him – at least until he could discover how to prise it out. But you had the key, Marcus. Do you realise what is was?'

'Key?' answered Marcus. 'No, I don't think so.'

'And if I told you that the creatures of the Dark never rest, could you guess then?'

Marcus thought for a moment. He looked back at Marchman, with surprise and confusion written large across his face.

'You mean, I – I'm . . .'

'Precisely, Marcus. You are asleep! Not here, on Galidian, of course. It was the only way to make sure that no-one from the Darkness could ever unlock it. The only problem I had was to pass the key on, so to speak. Case brought you to Galidian because I asked him to, although he didn't realise at the time that is was me directing his thoughts. That is why he couldn't tell you precisely why you were here. He didn't know. The Albard did the rest, finding the sphere and taking it to Stonefort. The first

160

group, the ones who found it originally, were unfortunately over taken by Greblocks before they could get down from the mountainside where they found it. I had to send a second group to recover it and take it to Stonefort, where Case gave it you Marcus.'

'You mean it was you what made us go?' interrupted General.

'That's right! It wasn't easy though!' he smiled.

'There!' he said rising. 'It's time for me to go and leave you good people to find your way home. By the way, Case, you will find a way through the mountain, up there!'

Marchman pointed, to a place high in the Curtains, and Case's sharp eye took note.

'Before you go, Marchman – what would have happened if we had not found you?' asked Marcus.

'As Ben said,' he replied simply. 'All would have been lost! Oh, and one last thing – you will find that everything is just as it was before all of this business began. Both the Albard and the Brendel that were lost in the struggle are now restored, just as Jade was!'

He turned, smiling, to General.

'I cannot say the same for the rock worm, my friend, but nevertheless, take good care on your way home!'

Hearty laughter rang around the morning desert, with General chuckling good-naturedly with them.

Finally, he turned to Jade.

'Your parents do love you, child. They will be very happy to see you home.'

With that Marchman was gone. No-one actually saw how, or

161

exactly when, but it was though he had never existed.

Marcus turned to Jade, who was sobbing her heart out.

'You're not really an orphan, then?' he asked, gently.

'No,' she replied, between sobs. 'I just ran away.'

'Never mind. Soon be home,' he comforted.

*   *   *

After resting all that day and spending the night comfortably with the Sandroamers, they set out for home. The desert people guided them out to the edge of the Curtains to the north east and Case found the mountain pass without difficulty, just where Marchman had said it would be. It brought them down to the source of the river which flowed through the Brendel forest. There, Case, Marcus, Jade and Grobwold said their sad farewells to the Albard, Case pressing them to visit Stonefort before too long. Shortly, they were heading off, waving as they went, down the slopes towards the Albard Caves. There was an especially long and fond wave from General for Marcus, who waved back until they were out of sight.

A day later, the Brendel arrived in their beloved forest, eager to see those they thought they had lost forever. Before he went, Hornbeam stood in front of Marcus. He lifted one of his long arms and touched him on the temple. Inside his head, he distinctly heard Hornbeam say 'A gift from the Brendel, Marcus. Use it well!'

'Thank you!' he replied, puzzled as to what kind of gift it was.

Moments later, they disappeared into the trees.

The journey from there it was a happy, relaxed affair, each of them enjoying the rich beauty of Galidian with fresh eyes. After all, they had nearly lost it. Jade was reunited with her parents in Middlemere, throwing herself into their arms, all three of them shedding tears of happiness.

Case, Marcus and Grobwold arrived back in Stonefort just fifteen days after leaving Smoking Mountain.

That night, it was a tearful Marcus who, with Case and Grobwold fussing over him, was getting ready for bed. As Case suggested, he'd washed and changed back into his T-shirt and jeans. He slid his comb into a back pocket and climbed into bed.

'Am I really going home, Case?' he asked.

Case nodded, not trusting himself to say anything, for he had become very fond of the boy.

'Goodnight, Grobwold. Take care!' he sniffed.

'You too, dear boy – you too!' Grobwold sniffed back, leaving the room.

'Until the next time, then!' said Case, smiling and ruffling his hair.

Moments later, he too was gone.

For what seemed like an age, Marcus lay there. Finally, taking one last look around, he turned over and went to sleep.

Chapter 15 - Marcus Flynn

Marcus stirred, wide awake in a moment.

'What are you doing up there?' his mother was calling. 'Supper's ready, so get yourself down here and be quick about it. Your dad's waiting!'

That was enough to galvanise him into action. He was off the bed in a trice and tearing downstairs into the kitchen.

'Hello dad!' he grinned. 'Sorry I'm late. Fell asleep.'

'It's alright for some, Marcus! How'd the football go this morning?'

'Lost, three-two,' he mumbled. 'I scored one. A header, for a change!'

'Don't speak with your mouth full!' scolded mother.

Mr Flynn's mobile rang.

'Why does it always do that when we sit down to a meal?' he complained, answering.

'Hello! . . . Yes, he is – hold on a moment!'

Mr Flynn passed his 'phone to Marcus.

'Why is it never for me? It's Mr Henderson from school – he wants a word.'

'Ooh, that's that nice games master, isn't it dear?' chipped in mother.

Mr Flynn shot her a look.

'Didn't mean anything love – just teasing!' she giggled.

Marcus took the 'phone out of the kitchen.

'Hello – Mr Henderson?'

'Yes. That you, Marcus?

'Yes, sir.'

'Good. I've got some news for you. Mr Wright's just called. You remember him from the County trials – he's in charge of selection. You're in the squad, Marcus. Congratulations!'

'The – the County squad,' stammered Marcus. 'Me?'

'That's right!' Thought you'd be pleased. OK – see you at school on Monday. Well done Marcus. We're all very proud of you!'

'Thank you, sir. That's great news!'

Marcus wandered back into the kitchen and handed his dad's 'phone back.

Mr Flynn looked up from his plate, enquiringly.

'Good news, son?'

'I'm in the County squad!' he blurted out, beaming with pride.

Mr Flynn jumped up and shook his son by the hand.

'Well done, Marcus! Well done! Fantastic news! Wait 'til I tell the lads at work.'

'Very nice, dear!' smiled his mum. 'Now get on with your suppers, the pair of you, or it'll be stone cold!'

*　　　*　　　*

Next morning, Marcus couldn't wait to get out and tell his friends about his selection. They met every Sunday to have a kick around in the park for an hour or two.

At breakfast, Marcus was handed a plate of sausage and eggs.

'Eggsies! Me fav'rite!' he exclaimed in a strange voice and not knowing why.

His mother gave him an odd look.

'You've never said that before!' she observed, drily.

After breakfast, Marcus was out of the door and hurrying along to the park as fast as he could go, swinging his boot bag as he went. Just as he turned into the park gates, he ran slap bang into Johnny Prescott and Fred Baines!

'Well, if it isn't our little Flip-Flop-Flynn!' leered Prescott. 'And where d'you think you're going in such a rush, knocking into poor innocent people like us?'

'I – I, er . . .' stammered Marcus, his path completely blocked by the two older and much bigger boys.

'Lost your tongue, have you? Soon get that back, won't we Fred!'

Prescott took hold of one of Marcus' ears and twisted it, hard.

'Ow – you're hurting!' yelled Marcus. 'Let go!'

'Tut, tut. Where are your manners? Now don't nark us, Marcus!' he sneered, laughing at his own well-worn joke, 'or you'll be getting plenty more where that came from!'

He gave his ear another painful tweak before pushing him hard into the park railings.

Marcus stood before him, breathless and angry. He put his hand to his ear. It felt hot and very sore.

He looked at Prescott defiantly, straight into his mocking, bully boy eyes, wishing he could do something. Without really knowing how, an image formed in his mind of Prescott being chased by a fearsome, two-headed monster, covered in tentacles and roaring as its jaws snapped ferociously after him.

At that precise moment, Prescott's face changed colour, the blood literally draining from his cheeks. Eyes filling with terror and jabbering incomprehensibly, he pointed somewhere behind Marcus.

Fred looked at his friend.

'What's up, Johnny?' he asked.

Prescott, yelling blue murder, turned on his heels and ran for all he was worth. A mystified Marcus and Baines stared after him. After a couple of moments, Baines looked at Marcus, spreading his hands in a 'don't ask me' gesture.

'See you around!' he mumbled, before setting off after the demented Prescott.

Marcus joined his group of friends who had been watching from the pitch.

'What was all that about?' they asked.

'Search me!' shrugged Marcus, 'Come on. Let's play football!'

He paused for a second, reflecting on the word he'd just used – 'search'.

It had a familiar ring, but he couldn't quite place where he'd heard it recently. Vague and distant memories swirled around in his mind, but he could not pinpoint anything in the mist.

'Oh, well – must have been a dream or something!' he decided.

Moments later, he was off, playing with his friends.

Printed in Poland
by Amazon Fulfillment
Poland Sp. z o.o., Wrocław

53606007R00101